STORIES
A MO

M000077428

Compiled and edited by

David Beaumier
Richard Pearce-Moses

Stories by

Molly Hite
Kenneth Meyer
Dianne Meyer
Richard Pearce-Moses
Nancy Sherer
Kim Bogren Owen
Bob Zaslow
Van Peltekian
Tom Altreuter
David Beaumier
Raj Gill

Chuckanut Editions
Bellingham, Washington
2021

1st ed.

ISBN: 978-0-9860097-6-1
LCCN: 2021903166

Cover design by Joe Donley.
Type design by Richard Pearce-Moses.

Printed in the United States of America

Chuckanut
Editions

Chuckanut Editions
An imprint of Village Books
1200 11th Street
Bellingham, Washington 98225
+1 360-671-2626

CONTENTS

PREFACE

As the world moved into isolation in March of 2020, our fiction writing group became a lifeline and a family for many of us. We went from meeting twice a month at Village Books to frequent gatherings in Zoom. We continued our usual critique sessions, but met more frequently to spend time with each other, socializing and writing quietly together.

Living through a pandemic reminded us of Giovanni Boccaccio's *Decameron*, a tale of a small group that fled Florence to escape the Black Death in 1348 A.D. They passed the time by telling stories. Some pious, other humorous, and more than a few bawdy. He apologized to his readers for reminding them of the dreadful plague, disheartening to all who saw or heard of it. Even so, he promised that the happiness that ended in misery would ultimately result in unexpected happiness.

We, like many others, decided to follow suit with Boccaccio, putting the feelings of this strange time into words. Our initial prompt was that the stories should entertain and amuse. *Do the stories have to relate to the pandemic?* No. They can be about anything, any genre. *Should they be funny, envisioning a happier future to keep people's spirits up?* No. They should reflect the author's experience, good or bad, hopeful or tragic. *Should they have an arc, be connected to each other?* No. The stories reflect our separation.

We are grateful to everyone who made this possible. The authors contributed great stories and workshopped them into something publishable. Thank you to Joe Donley for his beautiful cover design and to Village Books for their unending support for writing communities. While we continue to write separately, our work appears together. Someday we will be together again, too.

— David Beaumier & Richard Pearce-Moses

BEES

Molly Hite

Melissa put her club sandwich back on her plate and waved both hands. "Shoo!"

Sophie winced as she stood and backed away from her mother. "I can't believe you do that. It just makes them mad. You can't just say shoo to a yellow jacket." She picked up her plate and stood up. "Can't we eat inside? Lunch on the patio is no fun when there's a nest around somewhere close." The yellow jacket was buzzing in her face now.

"You see? Backing away like that. *That's* what makes them mad." Her mother went back to her sandwich. "Of course, I do have an unusually high pain threshold."

"You always say that too."

"I inherited it from my father." Melissa took a bite that just missed the yellow jacket. "Even when I was little, I was never scared that some bee would bite me."

"It isn't a bite," said Sophie. "And it's not a bee."

"Don't split hairs."

"None of us kids have a high pain threshold."

"Don't whine about how it's not fair. Life isn't fair," said Melissa with satisfaction.

"You always say that too. I'm going inside." Sophie picked up her plate and glass and turned away as the yellow jacket returned to buzzing around her mother's throat.

She was deciding if she had lost her appetite when her little brother Nick came in. "Can I have one of those sandwiches?" he asked.

"I'm not making one for you."

"Can I have yours?"

"Sure." Sophie handed him her plate. She was pretty sure a yellow jacket had landed on the sandwich at least a couple of times.

"You and Mom were fighting again."

"It wasn't fighting," said Sophie automatically.

"About those bees. I'm going to ask Dad to do something."

"At least get rid of the nest," said Sophia. "And they're not bees."

"He'll get the people from the association to get rid of the nest. They'll squirt it with something."

Sophie shrugged, wondering if she should say any more to Nick. He reported back to their parents. His big brother Aiden was worse. Aiden was working hard at being Dad's favorite. Now that he was eleven he and Dad were having these *serious* conversations where Aiden would look into Dad's eyes and nod slowly as if he really got it. Of course, Mom was doing some of the same stuff with her, wasn't she? Trying to turn her into somebody else, some mini-Mom. Maybe she was supposed to work on having a high pain threshold.

Nick swallowed the rest of the sandwich. "You read too much. Dad says he should never have got you that iPad. You're supposed to be doing Instagram, Snapchat, like that. Even Mom uses those sometimes."

"She uses Facebook," said Sophie.

"Yeah, because she's old. But you, you're just weird."

Sophie had been suspecting lately that she was weird. She wasn't sure that she minded that much, but her parents might try to modify her. There were whole sections of Reddit about how when you became a teenager your parents might try to modify you into somebody you weren't. "So why am I weird?"

"You use your iPad to read—*read*, like, news stuff. Or even *science*." Nick drew out the word as if it were unsanitary. "Dad told me you're going to be a nerd if you don't watch out."

"Science isn't bad. You do it in school, don't you?"

"Yeah, in school," he said, as if he had made a point. Sophie went upstairs to her bedroom to hide her iPad and get her phone because she was meeting her friend Madison in the park. Madison, too, was known to read online news sites and even talk about them. Maybe the two of them would get into the kind of discussion where Sophie could bring up the hornets.

She stayed in the park until almost six, although Madison had left three hours earlier. The hornet story hadn't led to the discussion Sophie had anticipated. Madison had said "Ew," and then "Why do you *talk* about such icky stuff? People don't *talk* about those things. Anyway, I think you made it up." Sophie had offered to pull up some sites on her phone that had pictures, but Madison just said, "That's totally gross," and stormed out of the park.

Dinner was tense, even though Sophie had set the table without being asked and carried the plates of artfully arranged Colonel Sanders pieces from the kitchen into the dining room.

When Nick asked, "What's for dessert?" their father slammed his plate down on the placemat until a drumstick hopped onto the floor.

"Is dessert all you can think about?" he demanded.

Nick wisely said nothing.

"Keep that up and you'll be a puffy little boy. You won't be able to play basketball, soccer, softball—anything."

"Your father has your future at heart," said Melissa. "Don't you, Andrew?"

"You betcha," said their father. "Your mom and I have decided we need to have a family meeting tonight. Instead of dessert." Nick stopped looking at the drumstick.

"A family meeting is an excellent idea," said Aiden, as if both parents had consulted with him and he had given the matter some thought.

As if on cue, their father and mother both stood up. Sophie looked down at her pieces of thigh and biscuit. Maybe they would let her stay to finish. "A meeting about you, young lady." Her father was actually pointing a finger at her. "Now."

Obviously she wasn't supposed to finish eating. Or take the plates back into the kitchen. Or was she? It was difficult to read the silent messages both parents seemed more and more committed to sending. Something about her growing up. No, something about her being unsatisfactory. A nerd. She wasn't supposed to be a nerd. She wasn't clear why not. They loved her good report cards.

"Let's all sit down," said her mother, with a trace of the gracious hostess voice she used when her bridge club met in the living room. "Sophie, you in the armchair. The boys on the loveseat. Andrew and I will be on the sofa."

Everyone took a place, struck silent by the abnormality of the proceedings. The sixty-inch television was in the family room. There was no reason for the whole family to be in the living room.

Her father glared around, as if he had assembled a hostile crowd. He was looking at the two boys fidgeting on the loveseat. He seemed to be addressing them rather than her.

"I'm sorry to say that your sister has been spreading a dangerous rumor. I had a call from Harry Ogilvy late this afternoon."

Aiden asked, "Who's Harry Ogilvy?"

"Harry Ogilvy is the father of Sophia's friend Madison. This afternoon Sophia told Madison a very frightening story. Sophia said that there were some new—um—"

"Bugs," said Melissa.

"Flying insects. Very large ones. *Giant* flying insects."

"Shit," said Aiden, and got a stern look from his father.

"Yes, it's a scary idea. You can see how it could make people very worried. Furthermore, these insects are supposed to have very, um, large stingers. Imagine if that was really happening."

"I don't see why anyone would worry," said their mother. "They're just big bees. We had big black bees at the summer house three or four years ago. They just burrowed into the wood around the door and never bit anybody, just chased away the wasps and yellow jackets. I kind of got to like them."

"Sophie wasn't talking about those bees," her father said.

"The ones I was talking about are hornets," said Sophie. "Some people call them Murder Hornets."

"Cool," said Nick.

Her father scowled in disapproval. "Just listen to that name. Murder Hornets. I happen to know they're getting a lot of publicity some places. Not legitimate places. Those internet sites. Probably black sites. Some of the tech guys in the office are talking about them. The sites and the bees, both. Tech guys are supposed to be smart, but you know, they don't have common sense. That's what's important when you hear stories about insects murdering somebody, common sense."

Nick inched forward on the loveseat. "Like, they're really supposed to murder people?"

"Sometimes they kill people," Sophie said helpfully. "Although I've only seen videos of them stinging rats. To death. They definitely kill rats."

Her father "Think about it, young lady. Doesn't that sound like science fiction? I mean, presuming there are these hornets and even that they're bigger than, um, normal, we know of no flying insects that carry that kind of menace for human beings or even their pets. So. Science fiction, where a few new bugs show up around here and people begin to get hysterical. You should know better than to believe them."

Aiden cleared his throat. "It's more like fantasy, actually. You see, there's science fiction and then there's fantasy. They're alike in some ways, but they're also different. For instance, science fiction would be more like big hornets from outer space."

"That would be amazing," said Nick.

"They're not from outer space," said her father. "Although I wouldn't be surprised if some of the so-called scientists we hear from decided to claim they were. You can't believe stuff

that you read on the internet. Good God, it's the very definition of fake science."

Melissa clasped his shoulder. "What kind of scientists, Andrew?"

"I don't know. Bug specialists."

"Entomologists," said Sophie.

Melissa sighed. "Honey, you've really got to stop reading
all that nonsense. Your father and I are worried you're going
down the, you know, wrong path."

"I read articles," said Sophia. "I'm not planning to be a
prostitute."

"Watch your mouth," said her father. "Anyway, you've
fallen for a story that's just a made-up nightmare. You're
young, so I can see how that might happen. But now you've
spread the story all over the neighborhood. Can you see how
that looks to other people? Madison has been in tears for hours
now. And she called up a bunch of your friends and told them
what you told her. That's really unforgivable."

Sophie was getting tired of this discussion. "I don't see
why," she said. "It's really happening. There are pictures and
videos online."

Nick and Aiden chorused "Where?"

"Google them. Giant Asian Hornets."

Both boys had their phones out when Andrew shouted,
"Put those down this minute. Do I have to take away everyone's devices?"

Melissa leaned toward the armchair. "When you say it's really happening, what do you mean, dear?"

Sophie said, "I mean it's getting to be a really big story.
There are more and more of the hornets. They're coming over

to settle here, places like this especially, in the Pacific Northwest, finally maybe the whole country."

"Bilge," said her father crisply. "You have to learn that not everything on the internet is true. You're supposed to know that by now."

"It was the *New York Times* site."

"They can be wrong," said her mother. "They aren't scientists, they just write things. How would they know about bugs?" She turned to her husband. "Just trying to help."

"They quote a lot of scientists. Entomologists and other specialists. They're really interested in these hornets. Giant Asian Hornets."

"That's such a cliché." Her father looked even angrier. "Anyway, do you know about fake science? A lot of science is fake. It's just made up to get reported on in places like the *New York Times*."

"Why?" her mother asked. "I mean, not that I don't think you're absolutely right, Andrew, but why do scientists fake their stories?"

"Money!" Her father looked smug. "They just want our money. *Our* money, because you know where that money comes from?

Aiden leaned forward too. "The government?"

His father clapped his hands. "Right the first time. And where does the government get its money?"

"Taxes," said Aiden. He knew this answer from other man-to-man talks with his father.

"Got it again," said Andrew. "You know, I think you're going to be the smart one in this family."

Sophia felt as if she had been slapped. "So what do you want me to do? Apologize to everybody?"

"Damn right," said her father. "And also tell them you got carried away. Just like a whole bunch of people in this country get carried away all the time. They hear some tale of woe, some story about how bad things are happening, and they lose their sense of proportion. That's what people in this country need. Proportion."

"Common sense too," said Aiden.

"Luckily, people like us know better. We know they're just bugs. Flying, stinging bugs for sure, but we should never doubt we can handle them. We Americans, human beings, we've handled a lot worse things."

"We've got rid of a lot of bugs recently," said Melissa. "I mean, there are a lot less bees than there used to be. If we can wipe out bees we can wipe out these Asian things."

Sophie couldn't stop herself. "Bees are good. They pollinate plants. Losing bees means our food sources are in jeopardy. And these hornets, among other things they eat bees. Honey bees."

"Enough," her father said. "Now you're picking up sayings like 'in jeopardy.' That's the way fake news writers write. Overdone. Now you and I are going to make a list of all the people Madison told about your scary story. And you're going to call them. All right?"

Sophia nodded. He wasn't as damaging as he could have been. At least he hadn't said anything about taking away the iPad.

* * *

Over the next month, she wondered if her father remembered he had made her phone all the people Madison had talked to. Nobody seemed to think the Murder Hornet story was a big deal. Mentions of the insects occasionally turned up on the local evening news, but the coverage was all reassuring, with experts shaking their heads at the idea that an educated public could take seriously anything called a Murder Hornet. Her father said "You see?" every time he joined her in front of the television. She reflected that the business of learning proportion was limiting a great deal that she found interesting in life. When media stories about the hornets began to get more frequent, no one seemed dedicated to provoking a panic, as her father had warned. She wondered sometimes what kind of news *would* provoke a panic. For example, many reports noted that the hornets were getting larger rather rapidly, but others emphasized that there were so many differences in the available information that experts—entomologists, she assumed—really couldn't arrive at usable data. Were the hornets really bigger, or were different people using different measurements? If the hornets *were* bigger, would that be an instance of very rapid evolution or were they getting better nourishment here in the Pacific Northwest, since it seemed to be a matter of agreement that people in China or, oh, India, for instance, weren't very well nourished? Then again, how was a flying insect getting across the Pacific Ocean? Was that even possible? Maybe the hornets were really small birds migrating; everyone knew birds migrated long distances.

"You'll notice that no one we know has actually seen one of these so-called insects," her father said as she was sitting in the corner of the sofa with her iPad.

"Maybe no one we know yet, but citizen scientists around here are trapping them in glass tubes and then gassing them. Almost all the hornets they capture are from around here. This county. That's kind of interesting. Why here? Then once the hornets are dead, the scientists measure them. So they have information. It's just... she felt for the word. "Ambiguous? Like, a lot of them at first were about two inches long, which is still big for a flying insect. But very soon some of them were three inchers. Imagine."

Her father muttered, "And what, pray tell, is a citizen scientist?"

"Oh, it's somebody interested in watching some species. Like a lot of people around here watch birds and make notes on them. Sometimes the notes go to the county agent's office."

"So we're getting our data from amateurs. And none of them are even people we know."

"Madison saw one last week," said Sophie, slipping her iPad behind her on the sofa. "She just totally freaked out. And she was the one saying I made it all up."

"Hmm," said her father. "Saw one what? And are you sure?"

"Her mom and dad have her seeing a doctor. You know, to find out if she's living in reality? She's talking to me again though. She said the thing was really horrible, big sticking out of an orange head and a long, long striped body with a great big stinger—"

"That hardly qualifies as evidence that these things actually exist."

"What about videos? There are a lot of videos online. You're still refusing to look at them—"

"I certainly am refusing," said her father. "People can alter so-called videos, make them into just about anything. I don't have time to waste on horror films. And I'm not sure why you have time. You should be thinking about your future."

Sophie was uneasy with the new line her parents were taking on her future. They seemed to want her to be like her dad. Sometimes at the dinner table he would clear his throat and say, "Oh, by the way," and then he would tell everybody for what seemed like hours about a new case he had. As far as she could tell, being a lawyer was a lot like their conversations about Murder Hornets. His job seemed to be explaining why something wasn't true. All things considered, she thought she would prefer being like her mother, who taught Zumba at the athletic club.

Autumn set in several weeks later. After they got back from school, Sophie and Nick sat on the back porch watching the sky darken, drinking lemonade, ignoring the yellow jackets, and talking about the hornets. "The bigger ones are the queens," she told Nick. "That makes sense, of course. It also means that the hornets are bringing their nests with them. A queen is necessary for a hive, or whatever you end up calling a Giant Asian Hornet's living place. A queen means they're breeding. That isn't good no matter what else is going on with them. There's also the increase in size. Three inches is a lot. I'll show you." She spread two fingers and pointed to the space between them.

"Holy shit," said Nick.

"You're getting worse," she said. "You saw what happened to me. Dad's getting less and less tolerant when we use adult language."

"Dad uses it," said Nick. "That's not fair."

Sophie repressed her automatic response that life isn't fair. That was her mother's line. "It's really not fair," she agreed.

"So what do we do if we see a—an Asian hornet?"

"They're not writing about that. They are—" she pulls in her breath "—conspicuously not writing about that."

"What's conspicuously?"

"It means you notice it. Which a lot of people are doing, I think, looking for practical information and not finding it. My first question is do I run like hell or stay still and hope it thinks I'm a tree? Which is problematic all by itself because I think they burrow into trees. I'm not sure. They have their nests in all kinds of places, mostly in forests. Which means parks. Even city parks. That's where they're being trapped, as far as I can tell. But what do you *do*?"

Nick waved his hand at the evergreen border of the back yard. "They could be right in there." They both stared at the trees. "I guess one thing you can do is stay away from trees."

"Hard out here." Sophia finished her lemonade and waved at the yellow jacket circulating around the top of the glass. "Funny, isn't it, how we almost don't mind the yellow jackets any more. If they sting you, you just say ow. I mean, it hurts for a while, and it really, really hurts, but you don't wonder if it can kill you."

"If you have an allergy it could," said Nick. "Ryan Mellors has an allergy to bee stings. He has to carry this medicine around with him and take it really fast if a bee gets him."

"Not a bee," says Sophia. "More like a yellow jacket or a wasp."

"Some are bees."

"Those aren't the ones we're worried about."

"We *are* worried," said Nick. "Conspicuously. Don't tell Dad."

Three more weeks later they were drinking lemonade again, but inside, at the kitchen table, looking out at the withering roses in their mother's flower bed. "It's fall and I haven't seen a Murder Hornet yet," said Nick.

"I keep reading about them getting trapped in the parks," said Sophie. "And Madison has seen another hornet. Her parents still have her in therapy."

"I haven't been seeing yellow jackets either," said Nick. "That's good, isn't it?"

"Maybe."

"You think the association squirted their nest?"

"I don't think so," said Sophie. "I don't think they're using pesticides any more. They're bad for—" She stopped before she said the word environment. Nick still reported everything she said to their parents. Her father had already snarled that she was getting to be like that crazy little nutcase Greta Whatsername. "Pesticides can give you cancer," she finished.

"Cancer is for old people," said Nick.

"Not all the time. You've seen videos of little kids in wheelchairs with bald heads. They have cancer."

"I have very thick hair," said Nick.

Sophie decided not to follow up this line of reasoning. "I meant it might not be pesticides that have killed the yellow jackets. It could be a new predator."

Nick stopped running his fingers through his hair. "You mean the hornets. I do know somebody else who saw one.

Liam Coleman and his dad were walking in the Railroad Park. That isn't even a hard hike. And they found a glass tube, not a little tube, a big one. Wide and long, both. Inside there was this orange and black striped body, really long, and a head with big, black eyes on it. Eyes that stuck out, like what you'd think you'd see on space aliens. Big eyes. The thing was dead, but it was definitely a Murder Hornet."

"Did they pick it up?"

"Hell, no. They just ran. It was dead but it had this major stinger. Maybe it could get you even if it was in a bottle and dead."

Sophie felt a tingle of anxiety. Somehow, having somebody you knew see a Murder Hornet made the threat more real. And more scary.

She worked at organizing her thoughts, at proceeding by logical steps the way a scientist would. "Did they think it was larger because it was a queen?

"Liam's dad looked up the hornets. Even if they're not the queen they're getting bigger. Something about how they do well in our climate. They don't like really hot weather, and the parts of China and Japan they come from are getting hotter. We're still pretty, you know, middle-warm."

"Temperate." Sophie got up to check the lock on the back yard window. "Don't tell Dad they left Asia because it's getting hotter. He hates that kind of information."

"It's not getting much hotter here," Nate pointed out. "Probably they have a lot of global warming in China and Japan but not where we live. Or any place in America," he added.

"It wouldn't be global then," said Sophie. This time she checked the lock on the side yard window. "You know, the hornets definitely kill people. You can find lists of how many people they kill in particular areas of Japan and China. It's more usual for them to kill cats and dogs, though. They have really poisonous venom, but it takes a lot of it, proportional to the size of the animal, before they've actually killed something."

"If a bunch of Murder Hornets in our back yard worked together stinging a person, the person would be dead, wouldn't they?"

"That hasn't happened yet," said Sophie, and then regretted that she'd said yet.

They both jerked upright as the front door slammed and their father shouted, an edge of apprehension in his voice, "Melissa? You home yet?"

Sophie called, "It's Thursday. She does Silver Sneakers Zumba. Why are you home early?"

"When does her damned class get out? This is important. Does she have her phone with her?"

Sophie figured this wasn't the time to point out there are no pockets on women's workout clothes. "I'll call the front desk," she said, but at that moment her father's phone began playing the chorus of "Smooth Operator." He shouted into it, "Melissa! Is that you?" A long pause. "No, listen, I'm talking. Listen, I'm *talking* to you. Just hold on." He turned and walked out of the kitchen. Sophie noted he wasn't quite steady on his feet. She and Nick followed at a respectful distance until he had collapsed into the Lazy Boy lounger in the family room. "No, I'm home. Yeah, I *know* it's early. Don't you think I know—Yeah, something's happened. Well, not exactly *at* work. But we found out about it at work. It's Rich Bryant. He's in the hospital."

Sophie and Nick looked at each other. They knew Rich Bryant, sort of. He was one of their dad's bosses. They listened to their mother's voice rising into a question, murmuring concern, then rising again. There was a pause, and then her father said, "No, he's not contagious, at least not in any normal sense." Another murmur rising into a question, which her father cut off by saying, "It was… one of those bugs. Bees. Not bees. Wasp-type things. Maybe more than one. Yeah, yeah, hornets. He'd been playing tennis, you know how Rich loves his tennis. They took him out on a stretcher."

Silence from the phone, then another rising sound, this one calmer. Their father continued. "Jim Federfield, that's who Rich was playing with. Jim said he was covered all over with big red bumps. All over his neck and face and arms and legs. And he was kind of talking really loud but not making much sense." A pause. "I don't *know* if he's allergic. It's not like a bee sting. These are huge flying bugs. Evidently they're bigger than anybody knew. Three, four, even five inches. Maybe more. And there are a lot of them. They're talking about an infestation." Another pause. "Infestation, as in a lot of them in the same place. As in disease. Scientists are the ones talking, who d'you think?"

Sophie shrugged. So much for fake science. Her father was shouting now. "Get here as soon as you can! Yeah, don't change clothes or shower. Just get into the car and drive. We need you."

He put the phone on the little table beside the Lazy Boy and leaned back. "Oh hell," he said. "Infestation. That's all we need."

Nick came two steps closer to where his father was spread out on the lounger. "Maybe it won't be around here."

"Rich Bryant was playing at the country club," said Andrew.

"That's not very close," said Nick.

"No, but—" Andrew waved his hand as if the sentence was too fatiguing to finish. "Not the kind of place you'd expect," he said at last.

Nick was going to ask why not but was interrupted by the sound of Aiden rattling down the stairs, then changing direction to burst into the family room. "There's a really big mother right at my window!" he shouted.

His father turned his head wearily toward his older son. "Don't say mother," he said.

"I didn't say motherfucker. I just said mother. Mother is an okay thing to say." Aiden sounded outraged.

"Shh," said Sophie.

"It had the most godawful stinger on it," said Aiden. I mean, it was sticking the thing through the screen. *Through* it."

Sophie ignored *godawful* and ran for the door. "Everybody, shut all the windows," she cried. "All over the house. Lock them!"

"It's okay, we have mostly those metal screens," said Aiden.

Their father seemed to have roused himself. "At work we locked all the windows in our office. The building manager locked the windows in the whole building. When I left, people were arguing about whether to keep the air conditioning on. Nobody knows what these freaks can get through."

Aiden eyed his father. "How did you get into the house? I mean, after you were home and had the car in the garage?"

Andrew rubbed his eyes. "Don't know. I didn't see anything. No big insects anyway. I just… walked up to the front door. The way I always do."

"After you'd heard about the infestation," said Nick. "You just walked in."

"Somehow I didn't think they'd be in this neighborhood."

"Why *not*?" Sophie demanded.

"Oh, just…" Andrew shook his head as if to clear it. "Well, we know your mom has a high pain threshold."

Sophie leaned over the Laz-Y Boy and looked into his face. "What do a whole bunch of vicious insects got to do with the neighborhood we live in? Or Mom's high pain threshold?"

Andrew straightened his back and took a deep breath. "You don't talk that way to your father, young lady."

Nick leaned into Andrew's face from the other side. "What about Mom?"

"Yeah," said Aiden. "What about Mom? You told her to come right home. You didn't tell her she was in danger, did you?"

It wasn't quite an accusation, but there was something in his voice. Their father blinked. "She'll be all right," he said.

Something might have happened, some version of a palace rebellion, except they all heard the key turn in the back door lock. Sophie came running into the kitchen. "Mom!" she cried. "You okay?"

Melissa, still in her crop top and leggings, opened the door a narrow crack and slid through. "I'm fine. How's your poor dad?"

"I'm not poor," said Andrew.

"Oh sweetie, you've been through so much. I was listening to the radio all the way home. There's a statewide emergency. It just… happened. Out of nowhere. And I haven't seen any sign of the bugs. If you ask me, it's all overblown."

"There was a great big one outside my window," said Aiden.

"Just one?"

"One was enough."

"Huh. Down at the Athletic Club everybody was talking about whether we should wear beekeepers' suits. Those billowing white things? I don't see why they all have to be white. It's not my look at all. Anyway, I'm not about to wear anything like that." Melissa nodded to indicate her principled resistance.

"If we wear something to keep them from stinging, it should be something more effective, said Andrew. "Serious. Like hazmat suits. When we heard about Rich, a few of us looked at some of the most recent photos on Google. Those stingers are way too long for the fabric you wear into a beehive."

"Oh, honey, they're bees, not bombs." Melissa patted her husband's shoulder. "Now here's what has been going through my mind. Isn't Rich Bryant the most junior of the partners in your firm? I've been wondering about that all the way back."

Andrew shrugged. "Yes, but he's just in the hospital. He's not dead."

Melissa smiled. "I called the hospital from the car. They're not letting anyone visit him. They do that when something is pretty bad. You know what I'm thinking?" No one said anything. "Well, I just bet he's got an allergy. Why else would he react so much to a bee bite, even if it's a big bee? But you can die from a bee bite if you're allergic."

Sophie was too glad to see her mother to correct her once again. For Melissa, flying insects would always be bees and the worst thing they could ever do was bite. She insisted on living in a less dangerous world than was currently terrifying the rest of the family. In a way, her mother was heroic.

"He might die," said Andrew, as if he were beginning to catch on.

"Well then," said Melissa, "Life isn't fair. But think about it: somebody will be promoted to partner. It would be a tragedy, of course, but you're doing very well now, and you've told me several times you're likely to be next in line."

"Rich is a good guy." Andrew's voice was almost a whisper.

"He is, he really is. And if something happens to him, well, that will be just terrible. But I've always said life was unfair."

"You have," murmured Andrew. "You always have."

Sophie listened to the interchange with growing unease. "It might not work out that way. It isn't just Rich Bryant who's in danger. There's a statewide emergency, you told us yourself. And Dad says they're talking about an infestation."

Melissa's nose wrinkled. "Infestation! That doesn't sound like our kind of thing, does it? How are these… these *vermin* supposed to be getting here anyway? Where do they come from?"

"Asia," said Nick. "Especially China and Japan."

"Japan? I've always thought of the Japanese as a clean people."

"Clean?" Sophie was puzzled. "What's clean have to do with anything?"

"Well, *you* know. When you think of infestations you think of, like, not very nice places. You know what I mean."

Andrew started to nod. "Like the Third World," he said. "Say, Africa. Or India. India has some nasty hygiene problems. Rivers with dead bodies floating in them. And there are lots of other places where people just don't take care of themselves."

Melissa was nodding along with him. "Even New York City. You know, they all have bugs, even the well-to-do people. Those what do you call them, cockroaches. Everywhere! You keep hearing about them."

Aiden cleared his throat. "Rats," he said. "In New York. Not to mention other places in America. Some places, it's like the Middle Ages. It's a known fact that there are rats in some of the apartments right here in our own town. Those places where people take drugs all the time. And throw their food wrappers right out on the street."

"And they don't bag up their dog poop," said Nick, picking up on his brother's growing enthusiasm.

Andrew was looking more alert now, to the point where he slid his legs to the side of the Lazy Boy and sat up. "Aiden only saw one hornet," he said. "People in my office were talking about a lot of hornets, but when I think of it that was just talk. Hearsay. Who knows how many of the things actually stung Rich Bryant? If he was allergic, it could have been one Murder Hornet. And what do you know but all of a sudden we've got orders to close and lock all the windows. That could be mass hysteria. I've never seen it before. I'm actually ashamed of our firm. One little accident on the tennis court and everybody's overreacting. Where's the evidence, I ask you?"

"You're such a great lawyer," said Melissa, patting his arm. "I have to go take a shower now."

"You've always taken care of yourself, haven't you?"

Melissa gave him a beatific smile. "We do in our part of town. You know that. We were brought up right. Also, we work out and we eat right. You look around some neighborhoods, you see just horrible things. People who've let themselves go. People who are just all fat and spreading out in all directions. Never taking a run, not even on easy trails or even sidewalks. Eating junk food, candy, takeout."

"We eat takeout," said Nick.

"I mean the kind of people who eat bad takeout. Fried stuff."

"I think fried stuff is okay now and then," said Andrew in his most judicious tone. "Like when the boys ask for Colonel Sanders. We don't go overboard. We don't deprive them of everything."

"In proportion, that's the trick." Melissa looked radiant. "Time for my shower!" She turned and bounced athletically out of the room. They listened to her running upstairs.

Sophie sat down slowly on one of the easy chairs the family used to watch television. "I'm not sure about the reasoning here."

Her father swung around to face her. "I beg your pardon? The what? The reasoning?"

She watched Nick wince and fold in on himself. Nick, who had been researching giant Asian hornets along with her. Who was getting interested in science. "I, um, I don't see why working out and eating good food have to do with not getting stung. Maybe sweating attracts the hornets, but—" She shrugged. "All this happened fast. And some in our neighborhood too. Who knows how many of the hornets will be around our house tomorrow?"

Her father frowned. "Just gloom and doom with you, isn't it? Ever since anybody heard about these things, you've been presuming the worst. And why is that? It's not like we've had infestations here every *year* or something. It's not like this state has a history of infestation. You just watch, these things will be gone in the next couple weeks at the most. After all, you told us yourself that mere amateurs have been trapping them and studying them, and if they can do it, so can the experts. That's what you've left out of your reasoning. The power of science."

Sophie knew she was supposed to be abashed, but she didn't feel like acting as if she were acknowledging the flaws in her thinking. She didn't see any flaws. She got up and went out to the kitchen. Above her head, she could hear the splashing of her mother's shower. She was reaching up to pull down the window shade when she saw a Giant Asian Hornet crawling slowly downwards, pressing its stinger through the openings in the metal screen. She looked up and saw another hornet above it, crawling downwards and stinging in the same almost methodical way.

"Mom! Dad!" she cried. "They're here! I mean, there are more of them! They're in the back yard!"

Aiden and Nick pushed into the kitchen. "Oh wow," said Nick. "Those are mega scary."

"The one I saw was bigger," said Aiden.

"I'm sure it's around too," said Sophie. "Who can we call? Who is supposed to take care of those things?"

Their mother appeared in the doorway to the upstairs, wrapped in a pink bathrobe with a matching towel around her head. "What happened?" she cried.

Sophie gestured at the window. "Look at that."

Melissa bent over and peered at the window. "Ick!" she said. "Disgusting. I wouldn't have believed something so ridiculous could be alive. Look at it! It's like a clown bug. Those gross colors and those eyes—how could anything see out of eyes that are just black? I mean, no pupil or anything. And that overdone stinger. It's like a Disney villain bee. I'm not impressed."

Sophie appeared at her elbow. "Mom, it doesn't matter if you're impressed. That's a Murder Hornet. It's dangerous. And there's more than one just on this window screen. We've got to be sure none of them can get at us."

"Oh darling, you're such a sissy," said her mother. "I guess I keep forgetting that I'm the only one in this family with a high pain threshold, but honestly, I can't see making a fuss over a stupid, silly bee. Or two or three. They're like they came buzzing out of a swamp or a jungle or even outer space, not a civilized place. I'm not going to let them frighten me. And if the newscasters or the Governor's office want us to act like this is an emergency, well, I'm not playing. I'm going to have a refreshing glass of lemonade in my own back yard."

"No, you're not, Mom." Sophie turned toward the door into the family room. "Dad, Nick, Aiden, please. Help me keep Mom inside," she called, as her mother toweled her hair briskly and opened the refrigerator door. "Mom, it's not the pain that can kill you. It's the venom. It's poison, shot right into your skin and bloodstream."

Her mother filled the glass with lemonade. "Nonsense. It's a known fact that people who die are often in a lot of pain," she said. "So if I'm not in a lot of pain, well, you see—?"

"No, no, that's not the way the logic works!"

Her father loomed up behind her. "Are you criticizing your mother's logic? What are you, a doctor?"

"Please, keep her inside. Oh hell," said Sophie. The door cracked open and Melissa stepped outside, pulling the handle behind her. She took a sip of lemonade and raised it in salute to the swarm descending on her. They couldn't hear what she was saying over the buzz of wings, but they could clearly read her lips.

She was saying "Shoo."

LISA PANDION AT STEAMWORKS BREWERY

Kenneth Meyer

3 October 2030

I was born in the last days of the republic

So began the proscribed novel of Lisa Pandion. And that first line alone was enough to justify administrative measures against the work: *the republic was still alive and well! Give me a break.* Karl Berrenger, a mid-level prosecutor at the Department of Justice, replaced the item in his backpack. He had already read it twice. It contained no surprises.

Karl's train pulled into Vancouver's Central Station.

And if Lisa wanted to seek refuge somewhere, why did it have to be this drenched city of absolutely no consequence. Why couldn't she go to Tahiti, or better still, Monaco—yeah, that would be super! And he would pursue her there. But no, owing to V29, the Europeans weren't welcoming Americans these days. Why pick on us… We're doing all we can.

Wearing his face-covering and peering irritably at his "Visitors' Choice" map, Berrenger trudged out of the station and turned north. It was sixty degrees and drizzling, which was about the best you could expect in this God-forsaken place. He could have taken the local line to the Waterfront station, but felt he needed some fresh air.

Lisa's novel was proscribed a month ago for unauthorized disclosure of classified information, and the author indicted for the same reason. The State Department suspended (not seized, because she still had it) Lisa's passport, and her picture was gazing combatively from all the border-post computer monitors, and there were plenty of printed versions of her image hanging from bulletin boards too. Unfortunately, Lisa did something imaginative and parked her battered ten-year-old Volvo with the ACLU sticker on the bumper five miles east of the town of Glacier in the Northern Cascades. From that point she hiked past Cowap Pass, proceeding north on the aptly-named Boundary Way, straight into Canadian British Columbia. That stroll also violated Canadian law, since the border was mostly closed now. Someone must have been waiting for her on the other side, since she immediately resurfaced in Vancouver. Karl wiped his left hand across his forehead: *the whole thing is like a bad remake of the Sound of Music.*

Two weeks earlier, her nine-year-old son, Brady, went to visit an uncle in the same city (familial visits were still permitted). Since he had made that trip two earlier times on an annual basis, no one was unduly alarmed.

Just before Karl departed on this mission, he was aghast to hear not only that Lisa skipped out of the country more or less effortlessly, and the son was gone too, but she also somehow wired out a sum of a hundred thousand dollars—or perhaps someone carried out a cashier's check, or carried out some bearer bonds—which sum shortly appeared in an account at the Canadian Imperial Bank of Commerce (strange ally for a decried anarchist).

For the Federal side, it was three strikes and they were out. The amount of one hundred thousand dollars was not a fortune, but it was a tidy sum. Since all the accounts of the accused were on a watch list, what happened? No funds should have been able to go anywhere. Had the Department of the Treasury fallen asleep entirely? Two FBI agents were also officially reprimanded in light of this fiasco. *The FBI isn't what it used to be,* reflected Karl ruefully. *What's wrong over there?*

The Canadians promptly did their "Switzerland of North America" thing and granted Lisa asylum. In Karl's opinion, they granted that request with unbecoming celerity.

Thus Karl's mission. He was to either lure his quarry back with assurances that everything could be smoothed over, or else pursue the soft line of threats: don't you want to see your relatives again? Your friends? Have a normal life in your own country? Eventually you will want to return, eventually you will face the charges, and so on.

The Waterfront station appeared before him: a bland brick building with Burrard Inlet shimmering beyond. Following the directions he found online, Karl turned right and found the Steamworks Brewery with a masked young Asian woman guarding the door.

"We're at capacity, sir," advised the attendant apologetically. A sign to the right proclaimed the establishment was following the twenty-five per cent seating rule. A few other would-be customers were standing about patiently.

"I'm here for the party of Ms. Pandion," replied Karl. "I believe a seat has already been set at the table for me."

The woman consulted her phone. "I see you here sir. Go right in. And don't forget to try one of our new Hazy Lost Lagoon IPAs!"

And keep them coming, thought Karl.

He walked past a long bar on his right and was directed down a spiral staircase by a server. There weren't more than twenty customers on the upper floor.

Downstairs it was dark but he immediately saw Lisa at a window—in fact it was the only window on that floor. You couldn't miss that mane of disorderly hair; *what was the Japanese word for that? Miridigami?* An echo from Karl's one year as an exchange student in Japan sixteen years ago. Two younger people were with Pandion, distanced per guidelines around the large table. One chair was left empty, facing the water. *Thanks for that. The chair with a view.*

He approached. "Lisa. Thanks for agreeing to see me."

"Karl." To Pandion her visitor looked tired and—not beaten, but resentful; either for having to make this journey, or for whatever reason.

"I wasn't sure if you would remember me," said Karl. He sat down and took off his mask, which was allowed while seated. Shaking hands was a thing of the past.

"Of course I remember you." *I remember you as a butt-kissing mediocrity,* thought Lisa. *And I didn't object to the mediocrity, but the butt-kissing was offensive.* "Law school and we've had the occasional exchange of emails… You won't object to my two chaperones, I'm sure. This is Charles, and this is Ginny. They're both students at UBC."

The two young people nodded but otherwise confined themselves to hostile glares. They were dressed in casual clothes. Karl wrote them off as utterly unremarkable. The one called Charles had a nervous tic of some kind that kept him blinking, as if he had just heard something unbelievable.

"Great school I hear," fibbed the visitor. Actually, he had heard no such thing. He knew nothing whatsoever about the University of British Columbia. The only point about UBC that interested him was that they gave Lisa a visiting lecturer position. If he were twenty, he wouldn't be caught dead at UBC.

No response to the great school line. Charles blinked.

The server appeared and Karl asked for a pint of the Hazy Lost Lagoon IPA.

"I was hoping we could talk in private," he ventured tentatively.

"I'm afraid Charles and Ginny are worried you might jab me with a poisoned umbrella-tip or something. You'll have to forgive them. They insist on staying." Lisa shrugged apologetically.

That was a slap in the face. She was comparing him to the Russian intelligence goons who poisoned dissidents or slipped them doses of radioactive materials! But Karl was not easily provoked—one reason he was sent on this mission. "As you see, I didn't even bring an umbrella."

"You should have."

"I know that now. At least I'm wearing the raincoat." He took that item off and hung it on a nearby coat rack. The IPA arrived and he sampled it. It was good.

"I was sorry to hear about your divorce."

"You mean from Merrill, or the country?" Lisa asked. Merrill was her ex-husband, also a lawyer.

"From Merrill of course. The U.S. hasn't divorced you. In fact that's why I'm here."

Lisa chose to answer only the first: "My husband said I was whining too much. And he was right."

I was whining, mused Lisa, *but Merrill is a defeatist. So I cut him loose. Disagree with me if you like, but don't disappoint me. It was like— which play is that? Coriolanus? Where the protagonist, being told he is being banished, shouts out, 'I banish you!' As for the 'U.S. not divorcing you,' Karl was going to say whatever he was going to say, there was no need to rush into it.* She doubted it would be earth-shaking.

"But how is your wife? Susan, am I right?"

"Yes. She's fine."

"Wellesley girl, I remember."

"Your memory is good."

I remember she was a snotty bitch, thought Lisa, *but: down girl, down.*

Karl changed the subject, moving closer to essential matters: "Congratulations on your appointment at UBC. I was a little surprised though, to see they have you in the Political Science Department. Your degree is in law, so how does that work?"

"Yes, I think it's example of the Canadian program to support exiles and refugees. As you know, the U.S. did quite a bit of the same thing in the last century, in the thirties and forties. All those Comparative Literature professors. They had to invent entire new departments just for them. I'm not sure about why I'm in the Political Science Department. But you know, right now I can't be choosy."

That was another slap in the face: comparing herself to those who in an earlier age fled the Soviet Union and Nazi Germany! It was outrageous.

Karl wondered if this conversation was being recorded. On his side the FBI recommended it, but he waved that away as laughable. If Ginny and Charles were recording, his words might turn up in some student newspaper, but who cared. Lisa was not going to incriminate herself, and he was going to say what he was going to say. There would be barbed remarks and hostility, and from his side offers of reconciliation or threats—probably both.

"And we didn't divorce you—"

Notice the 'we'. "Revoking my passport," began Lisa.

"We only suspended it," pointed out Karl.

"I love the new nomenclature. Perhaps we should both check the Federal code. I don't think there's anything like that in there. And then there's proscribing my book—"

"Upheld by the most recent session of the Supreme Court; justified on national security grounds during a period of extreme threat."

Isn't the gang currently in power is the most extreme threat? "A court which has been packed by the 'Reconstruction' regime," pointed out Lisa.

"This discussion is better than a class session," observed Ginny.

Karl wanted to tell her shut-up, but controlled himself.

"This is what happens when two lawyers get together," said Lisa mildly.

After the sudden death of the president in 2020, some citizens thought political life might return to general pre-2016 norms, but in the November election several state legislatures appointed electors who disregarded the emerging consensus against the incumbents. Lawyers of a certain persuasion argued that this was perfectly constitutional.

Last year President Meadows recognized several unofficial state militias—Lisa viewed most of them as a menace to the public—and authorized them to intervene in urban areas threatened by 'anarchist' unrest. By definition this seemed to include most of the U.S. West Coast. On the freedom of expression front, works of several other authors had been proscribed and in some cases the authors' profits seized.

Karl circled back to the earlier point: "You know, regarding your book—which I read by the way—aside from the question about the classified material, the action taken by the DOJ was merely an administrative measure, easily reversed."

"Karl, you've really found a home with these people. I wish you could hear yourself. You sound like Khrushchev describing a few 'minor measures' taken against Solzhenitsyn. Like forbidding him to go and collect the Nobel Prize for Literature."

Another slap in the face. Karl reddened but didn't lose composure. "That's a bit uncalled for," he responded primly.

While her visitor was collecting his thoughts, Lisa forged ahead: "We both studied overseas. You went to Japan, I went to China. At the beginning of this century the policy-makers talked about 'convergence.' It was usually taken to mean China would gradually become like the various democracies around the world. The wise men never in a million years thought that the opposite would occur: That the U.S. would become like China; a one-party, repressive state."

"Lisa, you know well the other parties still exist and are functioning."

"Point to Mr. Berrenger," said Charles.

"Cowed, heckled, splintered," riposted Lisa. "But I really want to refer to something Confucius pointed out—"

Confucius? Karl wondered.

'He said names needed to be rectified, or everything will fall into confusion. Names need to denote what is actually happening. We just touched on two examples of actions identified by misleading or utterly false names: 'administrative measures' and 'suspending' passports. I would also make a point about so-called Originalism."

This referred to the legal philosophy advocated by long-deceased Supreme Court Justice Scalia and contemporary like-minded souls that championed following the original intent of the founding fathers, and close adherence to the sense of the Constitution in its day.

The two students were the most attentive they had been since Karl walked down the stairs.

"The appellation 'Originalist' has been *occupied* by individuals with a certain viewpoint," continued Pandion. "But I consider myself to be an Originalist too—"

Karl *hmphed.*

"My understanding of the constitution encompasses acknowledgement of women's rights, no discrimination on the basis of sexual orientation, and so forth. My understanding welcomes evolution of legislation consonant with the needs of each generation, as recommended by Thomas Jefferson."

"That might be 'Neo-Originalism,'" granted Karl without heat. "But your *confreres* arguing from that viewpoint before the

Supreme Court have been rebuffed repeatedly. In fact, two of them are behind bars at this time."

"I daresay they shouldn't be."

"And as you know," Karl charged ahead, "the sentiment of Jefferson you applaud was contained in a letter, it isn't in the Constitution."

"Point for Mr. Berrenger," suggested the student Charles.

"He's still a founding father, though, isn't he," suggested Lisa gently. "No one has renamed him yet." She turned again to the two chaperones. Not without self-mockery: "Isn't this exciting? Two lawyers having a chat..."

"Oh yeah."

"Love it."

Pandion turned back to her guest. "Karl, why don't you proceed to whatever suggestions you have regarding my, mmm, situation."

"Very well. This IPA is excellent, by the way."

"You see? Vancouver has its attractions."

I wouldn't go that far. "So. The troubles arising from your novel are easily dealt with. All we want is the source of the material pertaining to relations with the militias. If we have that, all charges will be dropped. No one bears you ill-will because of your political views.

Oh sure. "Counselor, my work is a piece of fiction, as I have stated repeatedly."

"Eventually you'll have to come back to face the charges. Permit me to state, we already have an idea who your sources were. We merely need corroboration."

Pandion laughed. "Counselor, we've both worked as public prosecutors, so please spare me that line." *Which is bull.*

Berrenger was almost out of steam. The fact of the matter was, the book had given Pandion a certain notoriety. She wasn't just some kook in woods hanging out a sign that said, 'Oppose the government!' And she knew the law, and worse, how the law was used. Since she was granted asylum, there wasn't going to be any extradition. Short of going the Russian route, she would remain perched here in Vancouver, teaching whatever. She was divorced from the husband, and her boy was with her.

"This is so unnecessary. And eventually, you'll want to return home."

"I expect to. I expect to."

But the visitor thought he detected a trace of doubt on Pandion's face.

There were drops of water on the table from Karl's pint glass of the IPA. Not liking to leave a messy table, he dabbed them up with a napkin.

"I don't think there's anything more to say for now, then. I appreciate your seeing me. I'll just leave my card." He placed one on the table.

Pandion made no move to touch the card. "Of course, Karl. Safe journey back."

Berrenger raised his hands to indicate the two students. "Thank you for welcoming our author." He was good at those kinds of finishing touches. He assumed the two students were Canadians.

"We're U.S. citizens," clarified Ginny coolly.

"Goodbye then." *Best to get out of here. Don't drag it out.*

* * *

Berrenger retrieved his raincoat, paid his bill, and exited Steam-works. Outside it was still drizzling. *What is it with this place?* He would depart that same night, but there was no hurry.

You couldn't call that a success. The most he and Pandion had done was provide some entertainment to the two students. He and Lisa both knew what they believed, they merely reviewed it. He walked west along the waterfront past the two piers housing the Vancouver Convention Center. The mountains to the north provided a good backdrop to the city, but they were largely shrouded in mist.

Karl understood that some people viewed Lisa as a hero, but he didn't see it that way. To him she was just a trouble-maker; misguided, making a certain racket, but in the end, changing nothing.

Midway to Stanley Park, eight-seater seaplanes took on passengers at small piers and were taking off, one every ten minutes. According to the "Visitors' Choice" booklet, they were bound for Vancouver Island. The planes spiraled upward, then turned slowly to the west.

He thought it looked lonely up there.

IRA'S STORY

Dianne Meyer

My name is Ira Stone and here is my story.

The Arizona state highway crosses a dry river bed, cuts between two dry hills and twists up the side of a mountain. Until, just below the crest, the mountain swallows the road; and with it, my ten-year-old Plymouth Valiant; and inside the car, me. I am twenty-eight, a late bloomer with a diploma, Bachelor of Science in Accounting, dated May 11, 1980, seven days ago.

The mountain spits me and the Valiant out the other side and we descend into the little town, Pyrite, where I will work for a year courtesy of Nixon's Comprehensive Employment and Training Act—a jobs program to hire disadvantaged, overlooked, or otherwise not-first-tier-choice hires. Professor Altschuler was so pleased by my good fortune. "You played the system. Got your state-sponsored education here, now you go West and take over the tank town. Smart man, Ira." But I don't feel smart, pulling in at the first groceries-and-gas on the road downhill.

I feel panic. The air has no air in it at this elevation. Some chemical reaction between my sweat and the car upholstery has stained the back of my shirt the color of iodine. Also my left arm throbs, scalded red from four days cocked on the driver's side window. On the map it didn't look so far: a wiggly line angled down and to the left; west of Philadelphia, lots of room between one dot with a name and another dot with a name. Obviously, I would save plenty on gas. Just aim the car, and coast downhill. So wrong.

Pump the gas, pay the man. A handy pay phone clings to the wall by the door. A phone book, with the heft of a lab notebook and containing all the listings for this entire county, dangles from a chain. Now, a stranger in a strange land, a son of Moses, I panic-search the book for familiar names under G, L, R, S, under W—we may not have enough for a congregation here—*thank you Grandfather for Americanizing our name.*

Monday is my start date. Right now, Friday, I need food and a place to shower, sleep, live. At the bottom of the hill I park outside a funeral home next to a realty company which, the owner and sole occupant explains, does not handle rentals. "*Nobody* handles rentals."

"So how do people find a place to live?"

"*I* don't know. Ask around, I suppose."

"Where can I buy lunch?"

"Ructions is open now. Up two blocks. Can't miss it, hon," and she turns back to her ledger.

Music, country Western, spills out the door and onto the sidewalk at Ructions. *If you're waiting on me you're backin' up.* "Who's singing?" I ask the bartender.

"Royce and Jeanie Kendall." He punches two buttons and the McGarrigle Sisters take over the jukebox. "What'll you have."

"Steak and eggs and hash browns and a beer, ah, Bud, and a couple glasses water."

He leaves, I learn more about his musical tastes. When he returns and slides the plate and glasses and bottles of hot sauce across the counter, he catches sight of my left arm. His eyebrows go back. Our eyes meet.

"New York. I thought the drive would be easy. Four days."

"Aah. How long you plan to visit?"

"I have a job offer."

"Bullshit. There aren't any jobs."

"Sorry to hear that."

He returns to the kitchen. I land on the hash browns and watch via the pass-through as he maneuvers a mop over the floor. Then he wipes his hands down his apron and strolls up front. "Okay, I'm curious, where's this job you think you have?"

"City Hall."

He raises his eyes to heaven. "Aah! Backbiting, scandals, turnover, an election coming up! That's the good news. The bad news? The swamp cooler's broken, and—"

"Look. My funding expires in a year. I'll take it from there. Right now I need that first real job, also somewhere to live. Any ideas?"

"No... you solo?" I assent. He tilts his head, leans closer. "A friend of mine. Maura. Her sister Jenny moved out last month and Maura, she always needs a little more money, don't we all. She might rent out Jenny's studio, the half-basement. Nice old place on the hillside, windows, separate entrance. Interested?"

"Never hurts to ask."

"Here." He raises a corner of his apron, polishes his hands, flips my guest check over, sketches a map. "Tell her Steve from

Ructions sent you. Stop by, let me know how it goes." Steve pockets his tip. As we shake hands he adds, "And I've got a tip for you too. Maura doesn't date, you know, men."

Maura (barefoot, crew cut, kimono) is waiting for me on her porch when I drive up. We strike a deal; she even gives me the okay to share her kitchen upstairs and the washer-dryer.

She advises me to hustle downtown, set up a post office box—mail isn't delivered in Old Pyrite—and a local bank account. Then hit the MVD office next town over and buy an Arizona vehicle license plate quick, before the counter closes for the weekend. She loans me a screwdriver and pliers. "Don't leave the MVD parking lot till you've replaced it. Until then, that New York plate puts a target on your back, Ira."

I empty the Valiant, wash up, follow Maura's directions and then return via an alternate route, 'the flat way', she recommended. Avoiding the mountains, this road parallels the border with Mexico just a few miles south. "And what you'll see in the sky there," Maura added, "that's not clouds. It's smoke. From the smelter right across the line."

The flat way links up some outlying hamlets included in Pyrite proper. The dashboard clock shows ten minutes after five as I turn aside for a preview of City Hall: a thick-walled two-story whitewashed bunker of a building, with a dog asleep in the road out front. A flash of neon orange catches my eye on the side porch: prisoners.

Monday morning Tim, director of BCOP (Border Counties Opportunities Commission, an umbrella nonprofit across several counties bordering Mexico), is absent from work at City Hall, where BCOP rents office space on the second floor. My instructions are to check in first with Tim. BCOP monitors the CETA program. Tim is my information resource and reviewer.

Downstairs, in City Admin, my new co-workers are not eager to orient me. "Here's the finance office." A grumpy clerk unlocks a door, flips the light switch. This airless room contains two desks with space for three or four more. "Your cash window." She wrenches up the wooden slat blind and exposes a barred interior window opening into the front hall, like the priest's confessional you see in gangster flicks. "People pay their sewer and garbage bills here. Probably that'll be the first thing they make you do, print out and mail the damn quarterly bills. They're late. You're supposed to send them first week in April."

"What's that?" I blurt. On the wall behind us is an enormous ornate black iron door with a combination lock at its center, and a lever the length of a broomstick and three times as thick.

"The old Company vault. This building was the Company headquarters for the mine. Mine closed seven years back. Company's gone. Here's your key to your office door."

"How about one for the building too?"

"No. You're not on our payroll. Public Works opens at seven, they'll let you in. Usually somebody's here working past five. They'll let you out." She snaps on a rotating fan atop the row of file cabinets, leaves, returns. "You'll need this." She hands me a fly swatter and disappears. I begin by examining my filing cabinet—

Chaos! I flop into the tipsy swivel chair and put my face in my hands until the vertigo (heat? elevation? panic?) passes. *Be reasonable, Ira.* I'll make a new file system. Categorize by fund, department, and year. Print out a general ledger of activity through the year to date and cross-code ledger transactions to file documents. Already I know the fiscal year ends in June. This is late May. July begins with a new budget, and I must learn when we're scheduled for an audit.

I compose my face and return to the clerk in Admin. "When did your last finance director leave? I'm missing a lot of files."

"March. Left a big piggy mess behind him. If you can't find what you're looking for in those files, well, I boxed up a lot of his stuff that was laying around and stuck it in the vault." She heaves out of her chair. "Oh, come on. I'll show you."

In my office, she squares up to the vault door, twiddles the combination lock. "Right here, taped on the wall, that's the code. Spin the dial from little numbers to big numbers… get it loosened up… stop at 27… turn past 44 one time, then stop on it… then back up slow to 18, hear that click? Okay, here's the hard part." She raises a knee, aims her foot in its wooden platform sandal and kicks the iron door frame while simultaneously wrenching the heavy handle. Stands back, takes a deep breath and eases the ornately painted door open.

I sense rather than see a vast dust-ridden vault like a pharaoh's storehouse for his sojourn in the underworld, with one small filthy barred jail-cell window high out of reach in the far wall. My coworker clip-clops into the gloom, flips a light switch. My impression was not far off; this vault is the City's attic, garage, junk room. Packed with treasures and trash, it extends over maybe a third of this floor of our building.

Generations of battered file cabinets—from splintering oak up to tinny modern—cluster in barricades. Steel shelving like cliffs extend up, up, almost to the twelve-foot ceiling, and what do they hold?

Everything. Mineral samples, drill cores, broken machinery, machines in pristine condition, piles of crumpled rags, work boots, uniforms. Framed group photos and diplomas from one-day classes in how to be a more effective communicator, banners, holiday decorations stacked and strewn.

Foothills of cardboard boxes. Labeled, unlabeled, some with multiple and conflicting labels. Sun-bleached and crumbling ledgers and record books. Loose file folders escaped from those file drawers and boxes litter the shelves. "Let's see," my guide says. "His stuff's got to be around here somewhere." She settles on four cartons and together we kick-slide them along the dusty floor and ease them over the threshold into the finance office.

She stops my questions about how to use the computer on the table next to my desk. "Look, I don't know anything about your work." Then, "Okay. I'll give you the programmer's phone number. You can talk to him. First, though, I'm washing my hands."

Next morning, Tuesday, I arrive well before eight. Tim's in a meeting down the hall, Rosalie at the BCOP front desk explains. "They'll be breaking up soon though. You can wait in his office over there." I learn from Tim's desk and his walls that he has a blond wife, an Irish setter, a master's degree and is an Austin boy; maybe a year older than myself, with a career arc way out ahead.

He saunters in, tugging the damp back of his shirt away from his skin. "Awful hot on this top floor," he observes. "We try to bail out before the sun works over to the west side," and swings his arm into a handshake with me. "So, you're Ira, let me catch you up." He tilts his chin to direct me to a visitor's perch, settles into his oak swivel chair, pulls out a lower desk drawer, and props his feet in their tooled leather boots atop it.

"I want to meet our CETA students."

"Make that 'student'. One kid's family left town, the other one never came back after the second day. Only one boy left. His name's Berto." Tim watches for my reaction. "Nice boy, top grades, oldest child in a big traditional dead-broke Hispanic family. I'll be straight with you. You can't do much for him. Just monitor attendance and sign off on the timesheets, let Berto catch a break, collect his free money. Anything else I can do for you?"

"Yeah. I'm looking at work downstairs that hasn't been touched for months. I'll be here early, late, weekends, catching up. Clerks won't turn over a key to me for the front door."

"I'll send Rosalie across the line at lunch to run you a copy, she'll bring it to you."

"I'd be fine with taking the key to a locksmith in town myself."

He rummages in his cowboy jeans and passes me his keychain, holding out a big square-top key for my inspection. "Read it."

"Do Not Duplicate. City of Pyrite PD."

"See, the locksmith across the line doesn't read English."

Tim's supposed to be mentoring me. He doesn't impress me with his leadership skills. "Well, thanks. I'll check in with you again when I have a grip on the work in front of me. Meanwhile can you tell me where to find Berto?" Tim emits a small sigh. "I want a preliminary interview with him. Because I make progress reports to CETA. Students are supposed to be learning job skills."

Tim checks his wristwatch. "The drunk bus runs late, boys are probably still on the porch. Come on then," and we shuffle downstairs and across the main hall. "City's broke, see. So, short-staffed. So, they rent men from the drunk tank—the DWI center in the border town south of here—to beef up their work crews. City pays the prison fifty cents an hour for inmate labor," he marvels.

Maybe Tim notices my flinch, his voice takes on a defensive edge. "The year after the Company closed, town about died. Foreclosures. Men, families left to find work. Pyrite went bankrupt, came out of it, limps along day by day now. City's responsible for some beat infrastructure, and prison labor's a godsend."

I open the door to the side porch and we step into a jumble of men in orange zip-up overalls, with one gray-haired man in a City Public Works shirt lounging against the wall. Next to him a very thin and very tall young man, a boy really: T-shirt under a long-sleeved cotton shirt, wide-brim hat, jeans, work boots, a bandage on his forearm.

The jumpsuit crew animates. "Hey BirdO, here comes the bus! Gonna sit up front next to the driver again today?" "BirdO, he loves him some driver." "Got something goin on, Birdy?" "Cemetery today… *los fantasmas*," someone drawls. The 'drunk bus' which is a battered school bus hastily repainted white lurches to a stop near the stairs. Public Works steps up as the bus door accordions. The jumpsuits line up in silence with the boy at the end of the line.

"You Berto?" I ask him, and he nods without making eye contact. "I'm Ira Stone. With CETA, and I need you to work with me. Who's boss here, Public Works?" He nods again, and I hustle to the bus door and explain to Evans (the name on the shirt) that I'm in charge of Berto, permanently. Evans, poker-faced, climbs onto the bus and counts out the men and passes his clipboard to the driver for initialing.

With Berto, I return to the porch. Tim has evaporated, but he shows up a few minutes later in the finance office with a TRS-80 Tandy desktop computer in his arms. Rosalie, behind him, cradles a tractor-feed dot matrix printer. They place them on the second desk, Berto's desk, and hook them up.

"Use these to run your sewer and garbage bills. Pick up the floppy disks from the City Manager, he has the box of post-cards for printing too. And when you're finished, bring the equipment back to us."

"Thanks Rosalie, Tim. We'll do that," and they linger a while in the breeze from the fan before leaving. "Ever use a computer, Berto?"

"No. But I had a semester of typing this year in high school."

"Then you know the keyboard already. *Smart.*"

"Everybody laughed at me. But I didn't want to be in the shop class. Some people get hurt in there. Just like in Public Works."

We exchange what I call 'the look'. It means: *The world is hard, dangerous, unfair. I don't have to break it down for you.*

Together, Berto and I survive printing and mailing last quarter's sewer and garbage bills that week, then work the cash window when citizens arrive and gripe and pay. And I pester the clerk until she relents and finds another fan for Berto's desk.

Ignored, unsupervised, I create my own job and terms of employment. For example, when Berto explains how he rides to work with his father who goes on shift in the grocery at six in the morning, I set our office hours to 6 am to 3 pm so he's not napping in the truck for two hours, and his dad doesn't have to make a second trip to town to pick him up at the end of the day. This also means I arrive first to City Hall and hog the prime parking spot in the shade of a retaining wall.

I put in sixty-hour work weeks, reconstructing the current fiscal year, building for the new year, sketching goals to prepare for this year's audit (auditors will descend on us by September). Invite myself to council meetings, BCOP meetings. On Saturdays I rest and sometimes Maura and I have supper out at Ructions. Maura and her sisters sing in the Saturday Cabaret, the old bowling alley-turned-social-annex alongside Ructions. The girls model themselves on the Andrews Sisters. They call on me sometimes for backup, or special effects. I'm their 'biddi-biddi-bom' break in 'Bei Mir Bist Du Schoen'.

"We need to get out of this office sometimes, Berto," I tell my assistant. "I'm supposed to encourage your interest in job skills—obviously, we're doing that already—but also, you should see what jobs—no, what careers might interest you. You have a school counselor, right?"

"Yes. Ms. Callan."

I write down the name. "Yeah, so, has she discussed career plans with you? College plans? What's for you after high school? Have you chosen a major for college already?"

He clams up. This is the wrong way to talk with Berto. Reset.

"Berto. You're a good man with a serious mind. You will live another sixty years, maybe more." Pause. "You will support yourself, probably, for fifty years." Pause. "Most of those years you will also support other people." Long pause; Berto nods assent. "So, money is important. Also important, what you do to earn that money. The world needs you to give it your best help—the way I need your best help, right here, right now. Hey, I pulled you off the crew, remember? It was lucky for both of us."

Berto glances at his arm, where it's still pale from being under the bandage.

"Now, time to begin making your own luck. But how can you guess the way you want to spend your working life?"

"It's hard." His face darkens.

I lean back, jovial. "So, here's what we do. You have what, another five, six weeks with CETA? We make field trips." I straighten up. "Once, twice a week, you and I are taking an hour out of City Hall and going to places where people work. You walk around, ask questions, see what you like, don't like. Ask the people, how did they qualify to have their job? I'm bringing it up today because we're visiting the Flood Control office, County Building, 10 AM tomorrow."

"I don't know how to do this."

"I don't either, but we'll do it and get good at it. Same as we did here. C'mon, Berto, maybe I'll meet beautiful women, okay?"

Ms. Callan at the high school is not a beautiful woman, but she's willing to exert herself a little on Berto's behalf. We meet the week following and set up a calendar for Berto's aptitude tests, exams, college and scholarship and grant applications. I insist Berto needs every dollar he is entitled to from the Feds, the State, the university, also any private scholarships available. And I clarify for Ms. Callan that I will be an active bystander. Available for any references Berto needs. Calling her to verify deadlines are met.

"Why you?"

"Because I owe Berto. This is my first professional job and I couldn't have held it together without his help. Also, it's part of my job description."

Shortly after Berto returns to high school for his senior year, I'm back upstairs in Tim's office for my ninety-day review. Tim strolls in, checklist in hand, and we resume our places from three months ago. "Already got this filled out, Ira, saved us both a little time, anything you want to kick around?" He passes the checklist to me. I see Tim saved himself a lot of time, just checked 'Exceeds Expectations' all the way down the form and no additional comments. "Any ideas when the City's gonna fix the swamp cooler again?" Tim interjects.

"Yeah. 'Soon.'"

"Uh-huh, well I've got some news." He flexes his shoulders. "Got a new job and gave notice to my Board this morning, outta here in a couple weeks."

"Hey, good for you, Tim."

"You could turn in an application. Can't hurt—pays two, three times what you have from CETA. CETA's down with folks finding permanent work and leaving the program, you'll have my reference."

"Out of my league, Tim. You're the showboat, I'm the trawler. Imagine me building consensus around a conference table?"

He doesn't stifle his grin. "Well now, I believe you could learn, there's plenty classes BCOP can sponsor for team building, get you out of the office, make some contacts." Tim's smile fades. "You try real hard, Ira. You're a righteous man, but you sure are innocent, and that's dangerous. Here's a tip. If you stay in government work, best pattern to build? Never hold a position more than eighteen months. Show up, howdy around, work the crowd. Work your ass off for three months while you get the lay of the land. Ride it for a year and after fifteen months, get busy applying for a better job and be gone before shit lands. We're migrant workers, pal."

I can't believe I'm hearing this. Tim adds, "Ira? I'm not cynical. I have simply come to terms with life. If you sign your review sheet, I'll put it in the mail." I sign, he stands, I stand. "And I'll send you my forwarding address when I have one, glad to be a reference."

Elections bring in five new Council members and a new Mayor who brings in a new City Manager. Auditors arrive and review the previous fiscal year as the summer monsoons end. We don't have a clean audit letter from them; it's qualified, which means 'needs improvement'. Auditors are as unsure as I am if we have all the revenues and expenditures clearly stated.

Now I have a career goal: Remain with Pyrite through the next audit. Receive a clean audit letter. Exit Pyrite (remembering Tim's advice), move to the nearest big city, get a temp job while I take a Becker class for the CPA exam. Pass the exam. Apply for Federal jobs, stay mobile, head north.

Berto's returned to high school for his senior year, but I'm not solo in the finance office. Andy arrives and claims Berto's desk. Andy's name is nowhere on the payroll. So I ask him what's up.

Andy is, ah, a friend of the new Mayor, "From back in the day when Mayor George was a Company supervisor. Yep. I worked in this room for the Company myself, retired a couple years before they pulled out of town—that was 1974. What a Friday! Crews came up from the mine at quitting time, put their hands out for their pay envelopes and got a termination letter included, hah! Nobody knew that was coming."

Now he's here to help out Mayor George. A spidery old gent, Andy pads around in Hush Puppies, rummaging in file cabinets and cartons and vacated desks in the offices and in the City's great vault. He slathers his finds over Berto's desk, stacks documents on the floor around our room. I resent the mess, the stale dust levitated by our fans and particularly resent his habit of leaving the vault door ajar. It raises the hair on the back of my neck, particularly when I'm working at night.

There are ghosts then, trapped like smoke up in the ceiling corners where lamplight can't reach. I feel them watching me. I know they leak out of the vault like memories from the mind of an addled old man. I have nightmares—*dust, disorder, anarchy*.

But Andy, he's right at home in the vault. One day in late winter I run across him in there. He has made himself a second lair, a partially collapsed desk at the end of a trail through shelves and file cabinets.

He looks up, snaps shut the file folder on his desk, wheels around in his chair. I'm on his turf. "Mind if I ask you something?"

"Go on, Andy."

"Are you Italian? Or…"

"East Coast." I do the raised shoulder, the dismissive hand gesture, the head tilt.

"Thought so. You Mormon? Are there Italian Mormons?" That throws me. "Well you're always wearing a white shirt. Don't you guys have some special kind of undershirt too?"

"Don't know about all that, Andy. You got me there. Not Mormon."

"Hmmm. Then why…?"

"Just before I came to town I bought a five-pack of white shirts. Because this was an office job."

"I get it, yeah. We wore white shirts too back in Company days. But they were short sleeve, damn swamp cooler on the roof breaks down every year around May. And now? City can't pay to fix it till they clear the bank warrants and go cash positive, Mayor told me. Can't go out to bid till late this month! Hell, the Company, they'd get right on it. Send up a crew." He muses, I turn to leave. "This used to be a nice town," he says, surprising me. Because I've spent some time in the local library, and gabbing with Maura at home, and with Steve at Ructions. I know damn well Pyrite was everything you expect of a mining boom town: violence, taverns, whorehouses, diseases, capitalist oppression of the proletariat, riots—

"A nice town?"

Andy's old-apple face goes wistful. "Yeah. Sure wouldn't know it now. This was a good place to raise a family, good paying jobs, *safe*—everybody knew where they belonged."

"Hmm."

"Then it all came apart. Company couldn't compete with Chile ore. And people got to go where the work is. Scattered like quail. Then damn if a bunch of hippies didn't show up and take over Old Town! And all these people coming up from across the line and we're supposed to take care of them and their kids! Where's the sense in that!" His voice returns to a conversational level. "Company would've had a crew on our swamp cooler, same day."

"Say Andy, any chance you might put away some of these stacks of paper some time?"

"Mayor George, he's... kind of reviewing them. They'll be out of your hair, Ira."

"When?"

"Soon."

I glance at my desk calendar, a new one: January.

January becomes March. Tim's replacement at BCOP agrees to check in with CETA and arrange for Berto to return this year; I ask him to request a four-month extension for me as well, so I can clear the next audit and leave with pride. CETA grants both requests and March becomes May and Berto arrives. We trawl the vault and find a desk and table that can be propped up, and snag a chair from Council chambers when Andy's away.

Andy's displeased by our new roommate. He abandons the finance office and beelines to his burrow in the vault.

One afternoon I come downstairs from BCOP and catch Andy and the Mayor loitering on the other side of the vault door. The Mayor's face puckers to keep from laughing, while Andy, on tippytoes, makes kissyface to his fingers and wags them at Berto's back. Thank God Berto has a scholarship to State U, out of this town. I won't miss Pyrite.

Next morning, two men in orange jumpsuits arrive in our room with black plastic garbage bags, kneel on the thin carpet and commence loading the bags with the grubby stacks of old files and papers on the floor. Whoa!

"Those are City documents! What's going on?"

Andy spurts out of the vault. "Simmer down! Mayor's orders! You fellas keep moving! Ira," he turns to me, "Mayor George, that's one of the chores he gave me, cleaning out those files. He told me, 'lose the duplicates' because, as anybody can plainly see, we're running low on storage space. Out with the old. In with the new. Move with the times, Ira." He raises one Hush Puppy to step over the threshold, then turns back, triumphant. "Besides, you said to get those papers out of here. We're just doing what you recommended. I've got a witness for that."

Berto's rattled and I'm shaky. We go upstairs to the BCOP break room and have our midmorning coffee break early. "Let's think about something else. Ms. Callan, did she have any guidance for you about choosing a major?"

"No. She just asked, what was my favorite subject."

"And that was?"

Berto blooms. "Oh, geometry!"

I'm wonderstruck. That was my favorite too. "What made it special?"

"We had a good teacher, she *loooved* geometry. People laughed at her. But I felt that way too. It's so beautiful, so simple. It's so clear, and Mr. Stone, those Greek people who made geometry, they made something that lasted for hundreds, thousands of years, and it's still true now. How you take a hard question and find an answer from simple facts you know—it's, it's—"

"Pure."

"It's pure." He muses. "If only life could be like geometry... Come to think of it, your accounting, it's a little like geometry that way. You have simple ideas and you move from what's certain to what you have to prove. And it's interesting when you're doing it. People don't bother you, they leave you alone, they don't want to do the work. You don't have to lie or pretend to like them. You give them the truth because that's your job. Maybe I could be an accountant. Is it hard?"

"You could be an accountant. And if you change your mind? With enough classes you can have what's called a minor in accounting and you can always find work with good pay. If you're interested I'll bring in my textbook. We'll work on it during lunch hours."

May becomes July. After we run the sewer and garbage bills, and the first crush of payments recedes, I cast around for another practical skill for Berto to master, preferably computer related. Maybe something in the vault will trigger an idea. I cruise the tangled aisles between the shelves and file cabinets.

Andy jumps when I brush past him. He's lost, contemplating an old record book with a flaking nubbly black cover,

RECORDS printed in large chipped gold letters on its front and above in white ink and wavering handwriting, Pyrite Cemetery. "How 'bout this," Andy enthuses. "From the first cemetery, closed down, let's see," he leafs through the book a little past its midpoint. "Here we go. Nineteen-twelve. That's when the company took back the land and opened another pit."

He enjoys my disbelief.

"Well sure. You're kind of the finance director, right? So you must've noticed all those funny-size invoices we pay to the Company? For land rent?"

"I asked but nobody seemed to know what—"

"Well that's what I'm telling you right now, Ira. The Company, it owns all the mineral rights underground for miles around. Bought them all up from the US Government right after they had the minerals assayed. So everything you see in town? All built on Company land. You can buy a house. Build a house. No problem. But you lease the land from the Company and you owe an annual payment. So if the Company plans to mine the land under your house? They just terminate your lease, and—you've been past the Magnetite section of Pyrite, right?"

"Sure."

"All those little houses there? They used to be up on a hill where the second pit is now coming south from Old Town. Up high. Away from the town cemetery, that was a ways downhill. Don't want your water tainted. So the Company jacked up the houses, loaded 'em on flatbeds, rolled 'em down the road and got to blasting."

"My God."

"Well. It's a mining company, right?"

"And they… dug up the cemetery and moved the—"

"Yeah. Rounded up drifters and drunks from the jail and kept 'em busy. What do you want them to do, grow petunias?"

My stomach flips over before I can stop myself imagining what moving a cemetery would involve. Andy, triumphant, smacks the RECORDS book down on the shelf. "Good thing they got it done before the War. Afterwards? Spanish flu hit. Tore the town up. The new cemetery was a busy place, prison gangs digging, filling, digging again, my Dad said." Pleased with himself, he returns to his burrow. I linger until I feel calm enough to go back to work.

A second, smaller record book on the shelf next to Andy's find catches my eye. The threadbare gray-green cover is carefully hand-lettered PYRITE CEMETERY October 14, 1912–February 6, 1939.

And an idea is born. Berto could make a database for the cemetery, and visitors will have an easy way to find any gravesite they search for. Names, dates of birth and death, plot identification. Elated, I snatch the record book and bring it to Berto and lay out some ideas for this project, explain the concept of sorting data. And we'll have another field trip! To the cemetery and test the accuracy of information in his database! Estimate a margin of error, and—

And Berto is horrified.

"What's wrong, Berto?"

"You don't do that. You don't go to a cemetery for… *fun*."

Oh. "I'm sorry, Berto. You're right. That was a stupid idea. We won't do it. But a database, we should make a database. To respect the people who are gone. For anybody who comes here, looking for someone," I close my eyes, try not to think about the Old Cemetery. "We should do that. Don't you think so?"

He ponders. Finally, solemnly, he nods. We will help maintain order on life's and death's chaos. We can do that.

Early August we have a bright day after storms with thunder and hard wind, floodwaters rushing down Old Pyrite's canals, and a fresh taste like eucalyptus in the air. Just before lunchtime we hear the crash of the City Hall front door swung open wide, and there's a woman on our office threshold, her head swiveling side to side. "So this was Company headquarters. Oh my God, Marcie, look at the size of that safe door—"

"—well, get a snapshot of it and don't forget the flash—"

"—and a closeup of the Company insignia!" She enters, camera blazing. "We're hoping you folks at City Hall can help us. I'm Beth, and my sister Marcie, we're looking for your cemetery. Actually we're looking for someone *in* the cemetery. Lily Anne Mackey. Our sister." Both women with sensible haircuts and breezy pantsuits, brimming with the enthusiasm of the recently retired. I'm guessing, elementary school teachers, California.

"We're glad to look that up for you. We recently completed a cemetery database. Write down the spelling, date of birth, date of death," and I pass Marcie an index card and a ballpoint.

"Mom didn't say what month or day, just, 1918. In the flu epidemic that year, she said, winter, and Lily Anne was three years old when she died so let's see, 18 minus 3, 1915—"

"—and we didn't even know we had a sister! Or that Mom was married before! Mom was just full of surprises, there at the end!"

"Mom passed three weeks ago. She asked us to bury her by Lily Anne. That's why we're here—"

"—this is such a cute little town!"

Berto opens his database. We search for Mackey, trying various spellings. Then Lily Ann, Lillian, L. Search 1914 and 1915 as birthdate and find many 1918 deaths. So many children lost. But no entry that links all the data. Berto is humiliated.

"Marcie, I'll call Bill at the cemetery and maybe he can help us."

Bill's out with a DWI weedwacking crew, his wife says. But she'll track him down and he'll meet the sisters at the sexton's house. Sure, Bill can find a gravesite, no problem!

"Marcie, Beth, let's give you a city map from the visitors' table and trace the route to the cemetery. Bill will help you from there. Guess he has his own set of records. You and Bill can... talk over how to have your mother, your mother's remains—"

Beth smiles indulgently. "Oh, Mom's out in the back seat of the car."

"Her ashes," Marcie clarifies. "So we'll stop at the hardware store, pick up some things and change back at the motel, and get this done for Mom."

Tousled, red-faced, the sisters return early in the afternoon, this time in dusty new jeans and boots. "Well, we did it! And we left Bill a donation for the cemetery fund!"

"We brought shovels, all set to dig. But Bill fired up the backhoe and that took care of that."

Berto's face clears. A happy ending. It clouds once more. Our database is a failure.

* * *

Next morning Bill comes to City Hall to turn in the sisters' donation. We talk. Berto, behind me at his desk, listens.

"So, Bill, you have site records at the sexton's house?"

"I've been on the job eleven years and pretty well know where everybody's laid out. That name didn't ring a bell though. I thought it over, what I could do to make things right for the ladies. And I brought them to one of the common graves they used back then in the epidemic, if they had a lot of paupers or small children. And I told the ladies, your Lily Anne's right here. They left satisfied."

I hear Berto's sharp inhale. And after I run a copy of the check and our receipt for the sisters, I return and see Berto's face.

I have to ask Bill. "Bill? Was that really where—"

He cuts me off. "Now look, they're both dead, Lily Anne and her mother, and those sisters, they're happy. Honored their mother's wish." His voice drops. "Something else I heard? Company's opening a new seam nearby. They'll need our land for tailings. We'll have to move the cemetery and you know what that means, everything will be all jumbled up anyway."

I can feel the knife twisting in Berto's back. Databases? Accuracy, order? We do our best. We try so hard. *And oh, Berto: I am so sorry.*

THE NEW ABNORMAL

Richard Pearce-Moses

Nothing today. Nothing yesterday. Nothing tomorrow. After six months, Noah was done with isolating in his apartment. Not that he could do anything about it. The governor had extended the stay-safe protocols for another month. It was the third extension and probably wouldn't be the last. Other than a few quick trips to the store for groceries, he rarely went outside.

Not much chance for change anytime soon. Mornings he wondered what fresh hell he'd woken to, with news of anti-maskers, pundits, and politicians who figured protecting the economy counted for more than some old people dying. During the day, he doomscrolled through stories he'd seen a dozen times. Lies, damn lies, and presidential tweets.

People finally figured out it wasn't a hoax, that it was deadly, and the best way to stay healthy was to avoid getting together. Now, he found himself alone. His friends' obsession with how the virus had ruined their lives became tedious and boring, so he quit checking in. Trolls and bizarre ads had taken over social media, so he logged off for good. He'd occasionally crossed paths with his whacko neighbor, who told him to get out of the apartment, that he shouldn't be so damned paranoid. "Just taking precautions," Noah replied. A week ago, the neighbor died and was gone.

Ted was the exception. After more than ten years, the quick-romance-turned-best-friends had become one of those "it's complicated" things. When Ted moved, they meet for a monthly brunch. That ended when the restaurants closed. They might have gotten together in Ted's backyard, but he started working double shifts that left him exhausted. A phone call was rare.

Depression is anger turned inwards. He could hear Paul's voice echoing down the decades, a friend and Act Up! veteran lost to an earlier plague. Noah could easily handle the ordinary ups and downs of life, could cope with being alone for a while, but this was not ordinary.

He tried watching television and catching up on reading, but nothing appealed. The movies were dark and dystopian, the books were dysfunctional dramas, and the documentaries underscored decades of missteps that seemed to lead to this moment. Even the lighter fare seemed more snarky and cynical than amusing.

At first, he'd planned to make the best of the situation. What better time to work on that novel? After a month, he realized the pandemic's anxiety and uncertainty had sapped him of his creativity. It was a thing. Even the *New York Times* had diagnosed it as a secondary, artistic pandemic.

He wanted a release that would keep his hands busy. He needed something to do that might actually help. When the Lieutenant Governor put out a call for volunteers to make masks for front line workers, Noah signed up. He pulled his mother's ancient sewing machine out of the closet and oiled the bearings. It wasn't just altruism. The repetitive work was numbing and therapeutic, the pulsing thrum of the machine almost a mantra.

Tuesday night's trivia game provided an exception, a release from the forced solitude, a couple hours with friends. In the Before Times, he'd been part of the Quirks, a team of friends that played at a local brew pub. They were an eclectic bunch led by Mark, a retired firefighter Noah had met at a potluck. Mark knew Alex from synagogue, and Alex's wife Jamila joined in. The group knew a little bit about a lot of things. Except pop music.

When everything first shut down, that bit of family had scattered. Then Harold, the Quiz Master, took the game online so folks could connect. The Quirks were back, and others joined in. Alex's daughter Chelsey in California jumped in, followed by Robert, Chelsey's high school buddy. Noah recruited Ted for his knowledge of show tunes, disco divas, and foreign languages. His quick wit made him a hit with the team.

Moving from a crowded bar to Zoom had its ups and downs. One night the Quiz Master's internet crashed, leaving everyone staring into their screens with puzzled looks, the chat echoing confusion. Listening to Harold explain—more than once—how to open a link left Noah wondering how those people survived in 2020. Harold had some magic that smoothed everything out, an ebullient charm that helped people cope. At least the game never got bombed by some bot trying to stir up problems.

Back in the bar Noah hadn't paid too much attention to the rest of the crowd, and the teams hadn't mingled much Then, social distance had meant respecting a modicum of personal space rather than a six-foot contagion zone. Now, faces once on the other side of the bar were virtual inches away, scattered across the screen by an algorithm that was more random than artificially intelligent.

The first night, he couldn't ignore Mikey during the music round. The man had style. About forty with a sharp haircut and trim beard, great art and guitars in the background. Alone in his home, he moved to the music without inhibition, seeming to forget that others could see him. Flowing and graceful movements. Noah fixated on him, then looked away when it began to feel a bit creepy.

The fellow brushing his teeth maybe got points for oral hygiene, but what would Miss Manners say? At least everyone wore pants of some sort (or knew not to stand up while on camera).

QuickSilver had beautiful, brown eyes. In the bar, staring at him would have been rude. Noah pinned him, and Zoom filled the screen with his face, maps on the wall to his right, bookcases behind him. Too sterile to be a home, too casual to be an office. Those virtual brown eyes seemed to stare back, and Noah suddenly wondered if the fellow had some clue he'd been pinned, that someone had focused on him. Noah jumped back to the gallery view.

BeauxSmart was a team of three playing together that included a fortyish dad-bod who wore a full lumberjack's beard, flannel shirt, and a gimme cap. A woman and teen—likely a wife and daughter—were with him in a room with plaques, maps, photos, and who knows what other family history on the wall behind them. Noah was fascinated. The man exuded energy, bouncing around, clearly having a good time. The mom played on her tablet, and the daughter wandered in and out. He leaned into the screen, his face reacting to every question. A few times he jumped on the audio channel with a quick retort to the Quiz Master, but Harold gave him no mercy.

The games quickly grew into a ritual of fellowship and communion. The Nertz started wearing costumes. The members of Trivia Fountain made every Tuesday Speak Like a Pirate Day. The Quiz Master praised everyone for their efforts. He'd chat with individuals, bringing them into a virtual spotlight where the crowd could get to know them.

The game had been online for who knows… Everyone had lost track of time. Noah joined players who began to log in early to spend a little more time with the crowd. Seeing familiar faces gave him a sense of belonging.

One night, the dad from BeauxSmart logged in early, but instead of his home, he was wearing winter gear and clearly on a mountain top. "Greetings from Rainier!" came through over the sound of wind. "Battery in the phone won't last long, but a chance to say hello from 10,000 feet." He bantered with the Quiz Master for a bit, and logged off. *Who is this guy?*, Noah wondered.

The next week, he Zoomed in again as part of the pre-game chatter, clearly back on Rainier. Tonight the weather was clear, and he panned the camera around the valley below.

Noah unmuted. "Is being up there your job?"

"Pretty much," he answered.

Explains why he knew so much about the National Park Service, Noah thought.

BeauxSmart pointed his camera at the sun, easing below the horizon. "Hey, are you the one who made Harold's masks?"

How'd he know that? Noah unmuted again. "That's me. Keeps the demons at bay."

"Any chance I could get a couple? Those are pretty nice."

After a few hundred masks and a dozen or so YouTubes, Noah had figured out the basics of sewing, and he'd tweaked the pattern so they fit better. The masks were looking pretty good. "Happy to oblige. My neighbor gave me some great batik fabric, so I'm just paying it forward. Drop by some time, and you can pick a pattern you like."

"Roger that. Job's got me busy, so it might be a couple weeks."

"Any chance I could get another one?" Harold asked. "A friend showed up and his mask was, well... I told him to throw it away and gave him one you made for me."

Noah gave him a thumbs up, and Harold launched the game.

A couple weeks later, Harold gave Noah a call. "Beau's here. How about we meet up for a couple beers and masks?"

"Let me check my calendar. Ah, *quelle surprise*, I'm free," Noah said. "Let's meet in my backyard. Fewer people, and I've got plenty to drink. Come around the side of the house, and I'll meet you there."

Noah swept the porch and put a cloth over the table. *All is truly lost if we can't have a spot of color, a touch of luxury.* He was putting out a bowl of single-serve snacks when Harold and Beau came through the gate.

Harold was Harold, the same person online as he was back in the bar. Six feet of barely contained infectious cheer and optimism. Five minutes with him and all was right with the world. The same magic that made trivia nights work.

"Noah, this is BoBo," Harold said. "Not that you really need an introduction."

"BoBo?" Noah asked. He leaned into a handshake, then corrected midway to offer an elbow.

"High school nickname." BoBo pointed a finger at Harold. "I never came up with anything cute for him, though." He was even taller than Harold, a bear of a man. In spite of the mask, it was obvious the beard had been cleaned up. Shaggy hair still fell out of his green park service cap. From what Noah'd seen online, scruffy was chic these days.

"Haven't seen anyone in real life in weeks." Noah pointed them to the kitchen. "Grab yourself something."

"Whoa!" BoBo called through the door, holding up a ceramic bottle. "Where'd this Corenwyn come from?"

"A gift from a colleague in the Netherlands. Never tried it. Read it's made from juniper, and I'm a little allergic."

"Haven't had any since I went to the Netherlands a few years back. Mind if I open it?"

Noah put his beer down. "Brought it out for you. At the risk of being a little weird, I peeked at your Facebook page. Just curious. Saw that you got a Dutch passport, and I remembered I had this bottle. Pour one for me, too. Might as well try it."

When they came back outside, Noah raised his glass in a toast. "Eff 2020!"

"Amen to that!" they joined in.

Harold downed it all at once. It hit him hard, eyes squinting.

BoBo cracked up. "It's for sipping."

"Glad I got the mask back on in time," Harold coughed.

Noah liked it. A cross between whiskey and gin with spices thrown in. Definitely to be savored. Not bad at all.

"No politics. No pandemic. It's happy hour," Harold said.

"Does that include the apocalypse? I always heard we'd all be going to hell in a handbag," Noah said. "One of you know when those are gonna show up?"

"Lord," BoBo groaned. "I hope no handbags. I can never find one to match my shoes."

Harold grabbed a plate and held it like a shield. "I'm waiting for Captain America and Iron Man."

Noah took another sip of the Corenwyn. "Can we stick with Iron Man? He's funny, even if a bit snarky. Have you ever noticed that Captain America is a humorless, self-righteous dick?"

"Yep. Iron Man for me. I'm gonna go out laughing, if I can," BoBo said.

"Superheroes would be nice, but these days I'd be happy to have adults in charge. Sad that power's constantly trumping principle," and Noah knocked back the rest of the Corenwyn.

"Hey. No politics," Harold said. "We all need a break to recharge. Tell me something good you've done, something that'll brighten my day."

BoBo sat up, lifting his arms. "I'm psyched! I'm exalted! Sourdough disasters are history. Took a dozen loaves, but I finally got it figured out. Jenny and the kids love it."

"You should try it. Toasted with a bit of butter and honey, it's a bit of heaven," Harold said. "My good news is that Zoom released some updates that make the game easier to manage. Not exactly thrilling, but the less stress, the better." Nodding at Noah, "How about you?"

"Hang on a sec." Noah retrieved a small bag from the apartment, and pulled out some yarn and two fabric balls. "Knitted Knockers!"

BoBo and Harold laughed.

"Well, crocheted knockers, in my case. Hand-made prosthetics for women who've had mastectomies. My neighbor's made hundreds. I'd been making hats for homeless people while I was watching TV. When a friend was diagnosed with breast cancer, I switched."

"Show me," Harold said. He leaned over to get a better look.

Noah began adding stitches. "It's pretty much the same stitch. Hook through the loop, pick up the yarn, draw it through, and move to the next. You add some stitches to each row on the front, then decrease stitches on the back. When you're done, you put in some Poly-fil. Lighter, cooler, more comfortable. Or so I've been told. Not that a gay guy knows anything about boobies."

"You got any loose yarn?" BoBo asked.

Noah tossed him a bag, and BoBo pulled out a couple of skeins. He laid strands parallel across his thigh, then began weaving them into ornamental knots.

"Part of being a ranger. Crafts keep the kids busy and out of trouble. An ounce of nurturing prevents a pound of fussing. Learned the basics when I was a Sea Scout."

The conversation drifted comfortably. BoBo told stories of visitors vying for the Darwin Award at the park. "The bright orange signs say 'Danger,' but… There's always those few. Every ranger I know has a story. Or three."

Harold shared bizarre factoids he'd learned while doing research for trivia. "No one knows the name of Sky King's plane. That show's been gone for decades, but every time I ask the question I see a faraway look on almost everyone's face as they try to remember it, like it's just out of reach."

BoBo finished the bracelet and tossed it to Noah. "Gotta get back to the homestead. Up early to drive down to the park tomorrow. Thanks for the Corenwyn and the conversation."

Noah grabbed a bag of masks. "Take enough for your families and friends."

Harold stood, too. "Yep. We'll do it again. Nice to see you in the flesh."

"Amen, brothers!" and BoBo held his arms wide. "Virtual hugs."

Noah stretched his arms wide and smiled back. "Virtual hugs. Thanks."

The next Tuesday, Ted had a cough during the game. "Just allergies and smoke from the fires down south. I'm fine. It'll pass when the wind changes."

Wednesday, he called Noah from the hospital. "They're not sure. The test for the virus came back negative, but the doc is concerned it might be a false negative. I'm really tired and achy. A low fever, about 100 degrees. Cough's not getting any better, and my chest hurts from that. The docs say the virus symptoms are random, so they're keeping me overnight for observation."

"What do you need? Can I bring you anything?" Noah asked.

"Can't have visitors. Take care of my cat and water the plants, I guess. I've got you listed as my primary contact. These days, the Quirks are pretty much my family."

Thursday, the hospital called. "Your friend Ted's been moved to the ICU. He doesn't have a medical power of attorney listed. Do you know if he has an advance directive?"

Noah was silent. *Ted parents were dead. Ted quit talking to his sister when she told him the gays like him were going to hell… freakin' evangelicals would get there first.*

"Hello? You there?"

"Sorry. Yes. A bit much to take in. I'll see if I can find something and check in tomorrow," Noah said.

Noah sent the Quirks a text letting them know about Ted's condition, then left for Ted's house to see if he could find anything about a directive or someone with power of attorney. His phone started pinging with incoming messages on the drive over.

"OMG give him my love"

"<3s to Ted. Can I help"

"Are U kidding"

"F--- 2020"

Noah opened the door to Ted's house, mask and gloves on tight. Galena was at the door meowing. *Probably have to take her to my place*, he thought and sneezed in anticipation. In the small bedroom Ted used as an office, Noah looked through all the clutter on the desk. He scanned the folders in the drawers.

Nothing. When he leafed through a birthday book, a small slip of paper fell out with "CorrectHorseBatteryStaple" scrawled on it.

Not exactly a secure password, he thought as he turned on the computer. The password didn't work, but he changed the o's to zeroes and was in. *We're definitely going to have a talk about secure passwords, bud.* Noah began browsing the directories, trying to spot any health information without snooping too much. Even the closest friends had secrets. When nothing turned up, he launched a search for files containing "health." That'd take a while, so he went to get the cat's food and crate.

When he sat down again, the search displayed a few dozen files. After half an hour scanning the documents, nothing. Ted's fate would be at the mercy of the doctors and the legal system. He shut the system down, got Galena in her crate, and took her to his apartment.

Trivia Tuesday came, and Ted was still in the ICU and barely conscious. The doctor had told Noah there was still no sign of the virus. The test could be another false negative. They were uncertain about exactly what was wrong. The fever had gone up, and his white blood cell count was high. He was on fluids and an antibiotic drip to keep him comfortable, but he wasn't improving. "We've got a call into specialists to help us diagnose the problem. The silver lining is that the case is odd enough that it'll get their attention."

A nurse held a phone to Ted's ear when Noah had called. "The Quirks all send their love. Can't wait for you to get back." Noah heard breathing and a cough.

That night, before the game started, Noah messaged the Quirks, telling them what he knew. "Sorry for the downer."

Before anyone could respond, Harold launched in. "Welcome, and let's get going! Category one, Gilmore Girls. First question. Who sings the show's theme song? Off to your rooms to discuss."

Alex moaned. "None of us watched that show. We're gonna bomb."

Josh laughed. "My suggestion for this week's category was 'anything but the Gilmore Girls.' Let's just cheat and search the web. We can fess up when he announces the score."

"Nah, I don't feel like cheating. Just leave them blank," David said.

The breakout closed, and Harold continued. "Next question. What does Luke use as the logo for his café?" and sent them back to their room.

Jamila groaned. "Eight more questions after this. I don't know if we should take Josh's suggestion to cheat or just throw in the towel."

At the end of the round, Harold announced standings. "Team IZoomlation aced it. No surprise. They ganged up and all suggested the same topic. And we have a new first. Quirks didn't get any. Dudes, not even the easy ones."

Josh piped up. "Hey, Harold! I *did* suggest 'anything but Gilmore Girls'."

"Point taken," Harold laughed. "Now, something special for round two. Gilmore boys. Question one. Scott Patterson played Luke. Before the Gilmore Girls, what was he better known for playing. Off to your breakout rooms."

David sighed. "Folks, my heart's just not in it. I think I'm gonna call it a night."

"Me too," Noah said, and the rest nodded. "I'll send a note to Harold."

Noah pulled himself out of bed and poured a mug of coffee. He showered, standing motionless as the hot water ran over his head, trying to clear the remnants of dreams from his head. His phone pinged, and he forced himself out of the shower. *Might be the doc.*

Instead, it was a text from Harold. "U ok?"

Noah dressed, then sat on the bed. He swallowed the rest of the coffee, even though it was cold. He shuddered, overwhelmed, as his emotions cratered, feeling everything he'd ever screwed up. The virus, the isolation, whatever bug Ted had, the smoke from the fires, the politics. *No power to fight, no place to flee. I'm stuck here alone.*

"Thx. Worried about Ted. It's tough," he texted back.

Noah was surprised when the phone rang, Harold's name on the screen. Noah took a deep breath and answered.

"Sometimes primitive technology and voices work a little better than text. You okay? You need to talk?"

"Nice to hear your voice. The ones in my head aren't nearly as friendly these days."

"Tough times, and I won't tell you they'll get better. I don't know. I hope, but I don't know."

Noah wiped his eyes. *Deep breaths.* "I'll be okay. These six months have been an emotional rollercoaster. I do my best to slide through the slumps, keep busy, listen to books and music to keep the demons at bay. Let myself enjoy the peaks, even though I know they're ephemeral."

"Yeah, I hear you. My wife and I go through the same thing. Our kids know something's wrong, but we try to keep things as normal as possible. Whatever normal means anymore."

"Thanks for checking in. It helps. Nice to hear your voice."

"Holler if I can do anything," and Harold hung up.

Galena wandered in and rubbed Noah's leg. *Chow time*, he thought as he picked the cat up, cradling it in his arms and scratching her tummy. *At least I've got this love sponge.*

He poured kibble in her dish, then scrambled eggs for breakfast, wishing he was having his monthly brunch with Ted at Nana's Cafe. Cleaning up, he looked at the rain out the window. *No walks today, back to the mask mines.*

He turned the lights on in the guest room and settled down at his make-shift workbench. He plugged in an audiobook. *Moby Dick* seemed about right this morning. He could certainly sympathize with Ishmael's mood, grim about the mouth, lingering with a group of mourners in the graveyard, fantasizing in spite of his Quaker sensibilities about taking out politicians whose inactions and willful ignorance had led to the wretched state of the world. If Ishmael took to a ship to calm his spleen and circulation, Noah escaped to his Singer. The repetition of cutting fabric, making straps, and the rhythm of the machine was a balm to his soul.

Three hours and thirty masks, he thought. *Enough. Time for a break.* He'd been hunched over the machine, so his back was sore. He'd even burned his fingers on the iron. He stepped onto his porch to feel the drizzle, to smell the damp blowing in the chill wind. He looked up, and the sky was filled with complex patterns of clouds, dark gray, white, and even a spot or two of blue. *Might have time for a walk before lunch after all.*

A Mazda compact parked across the street. The driver pulled on a mask, then got out and started up the sidewalk.

Noah started to go back inside, then did a double take. "BoBo?" Noah asked.

"In the flesh." He stopped six feet from Noah.

"Wasn't expecting anyone. Let me grab a mask from inside."

"No need, really. I mean, sure if you want to. But this breeze makes it pretty much superfluous." BoBo zipped up his jacket.

"I think you're right. But I don't want to make assumptions about people's comfort levels."

"Thanks, but I'm good as long as we're outside." And he pulled his mask down. "Harold said you were having a rough spot."

Noah looked at his feet. "A friend's got something the docs can't diagnose. He's sick enough that I can't even talk to him. I'm worried. On top of isolation, I'm bored and a little whiny. I'll get over myself in short order."

"Got some cheese to go with that whine? It'd be good on this sourdough." BoBo stepped closer and held out a small package.

Noah laughed and took a whiff. "Smells great. Want some coffee? Something else?"

"Another time, I'd like that. Gotta run, but one more gift, if you want." He paused. "Hold your breath, I'll hold mine, and you get a hug."

Noah nodded. He closed his eyes and felt BoBo's arms wrap around him, bringing him in close with a hand behind his head, cradling him in a warm, strong hug that lasted maybe five seconds. Noah caught a hint of Old Spice, and BoBo's beard scratched his cheek.

BoBo stepped back, and Noah opened his eyes. "Thought you might need that," BoBo said. "You gonna be okay?"

Noah combed his hair with his fingers and let out a breath. "Definitely needed that. I'm not sure I can remember the last time I hugged someone. Months, I guess."

"Remember sterilizing packages from the store? Seems a little crazy now, but we didn't know. Epidemiologist I know helped figure basic precautions keep people safe. Fresh air is the biggest factor."

"Yeah. All the arguments over whether masks were effective, what kind of cloth to use. Sometimes I've wondered if I spent all that time sewing masks for nothing." Noah stretched, forcing his back straight. "I think you got some kinks out of my spine."

"Got some more errands to run and I need to get going. Oh, and Jenny said to thank you again for the masks. Made it easier to get the kids to wear them. Mason really loves the wizards, and Abby's all about rainbows. And mine! The other rangers are really envious of the one with dinosaurs."

"Glad they worked out. I owe you for the bread and the visit," Noah said.

"You owe me nothing." He turned and started towards the car. "I got these nice masks. I got a friend. And, I gotta go. Later, bud."

Noah waved as BoBo drove off. A little sun broke through the clouds.

Noah's phone rang with St Joseph's name on the screen. "Noah, here."

"Dr Michelson here. I've got some good news. Looks like we've found what's making Ted sick, and we're changing treatment."

Noah gripped the phone.

"Fungal infection caused by candida auris. Only a few scattered cases have been popping up around the world. Bizarre, too. No apparent connection between them. Symptoms aren't particularly distinct and diagnosis requires special tests. It's so unusual, there are so many other more likely causes, that checking for it was low on the list."

"I guess I'm naïve, but don't you just test for everything?" Noah asked.

"Wastes time and money chasing after things that are rare. What they taught us in med school, if you hear hoofbeats behind you, you don't expect it to be zebras. Starting with the most likely suspects gives a correct diagnosis more than eighty percent of the time. We don't go looking for zebras until we rule out what's more likely. Ted's cough complicated the diagnosis. Looks like that really was allergies."

"So what does that mean?" Noah asked.

"Took him off antibiotics and switched him to an echinocandin, an antifungal. I'm really optimistic he'll be doing a lot better in a day or two. It'll take him a while to get back on his feet. Sometimes the fungus lingers for a long time at a low level. We'll monitor him closely, but now that we know what to look for, we can manage a chronic case."

"When can I see him?" Noah asked.

"The hospital is still quarantined. I expect he'll be more alert in a day, two at most, and you can talk to him on the phone. He could be home in a week."

Noah knocked on Ted's door and used his key to let himself in. Galena greeted him at the door. "Good to be home, huh?" he asked, scratching the cat behind the ears.

"Noah?" Ted called from the kitchen.

"You were expecting someone else? A little early to be on Grindr, don't you think?"

"What, and deprive the world of this?" Ted camped a glamour pose.

"Speaking of which, got you supplies at the Swingles Safeway. Not that anyone's been cruising there for years." Noah put bags of food on the counter and helped Ted put things away.

Ted held up a jar of spaghetti sauce. "How sweet of you to remember… The first thing you ever said to me was, 'What do you prefer, Ragu or Prego?'"

"And the first thing you said to me was, 'Your place or mine?' Now sit," he told Ted. "I can do this, and you're obviously tired. It's gonna take more than a couple of weeks for you to get your strength back."

Ted steadied himself with a hand on the table as he slowly sank into the chair. "If I ever do. Every day, in every way, eff this shit. It's been a month since I got home, and I'm still tired."

"If you were looking for Pollyanna to cheer you up, you're out of luck."

"You're wicked and mean, but I love you just the same," Ted said.

"I'm right there with you. We've grown old together, an old married couple who were never married." Noah grabbed the coffee pot. "Refill?"

Ted held out his mug with a shaky hand. "Saw the news this morning that the vaccines aren't the miracle everyone was hoping for. Helps those who get it, but most people may have to wait a year. Guess those of us at risk aren't getting out of isolation anytime soon."

"At least you have a cat. But you're right. Looks like we're gonna be stuck in bubbles for a long time."

"So who's this BoBo fellow from Trivia?" Ted asked. "You two were really ragging Harold last night."

"On the BeauxSmart team. Old friend of Harold's. He found out I made Harold's masks, and asked about getting some. Came up for a beer with Harold a couple months ago. A kindred spirit with amazing energy. Nice to tap into that. We've gotten together for a beer a couple times."

"Sounds better than a cat," Ted said.

"Actually, I may be the cat."

"Huh?"

"BoBo asked me if I wanted to join his bubble. He offered to let me move into the guest house at his place. Little mother-in-law cottage in the backyard. Smaller than my apartment, but there's a great garden. It saves me money and they get some rent."

Ted put his mug down. "You said he had a family. What do they think?"

"He's had me down to his place a few times. Jenny, his wife, is amazing. A hint of earthmother. Works for the Department of Ecology. Some sort of programming-data analyst position. Son and a daughter, middle and high school. They've got their mother's smarts and their father's mischievousness. I've been helping them with their classes. They started calling me their fairy godfather. You should see them bragging to their friends."

"Sounds nice, but where does that leave me?" Ted asked.

"I don't follow you."

"You're leaving my bubble for theirs."

Noah reached out for Ted's hand. "Nope. Never gonna happen. You were part of the deal. You'll be part of the bubble, if you want. He knows you and I are sons of different mothers."

"They're not too worried? I only got out of the hospital a few weeks ago. Not to mention we've never even met."

"Actually, BoBo suggested it. And he's heard stories about us. He knows you've been isolating, so covid's not the issue. His wife agreed. Not worried about the fungus, either. It's really rare, and if they caught it, the docs would know to look for it."

"So you're really going to move? When?" Ted asked.

"Last weekend. And, you're invited for New Year's Eve."

Ted brought champagne. He pulled off his mask and gave Jenny a chaste kiss on the cheek. "I'm staying up to midnight to tell this year to kiss off one last time."

She took the bottles from him. "Veuve Clicquot. Nice! Noah's in the family room." She hollered at the kids. "Uncle Ted's here."

Ted slipped off his coat and shoes in the entryway. "Dom Perignon's a little outside the budget, and our friend Tom says Clicquot is better, anyway."

In the family room Noah gave Ted a half-hug from the sofa. "A pedestrian tradition for a couple of pedestrian guys, but champagne's supposed to bring good luck. Guess we should have gone for a better brand last year."

"That's why I splurged," Ted said. He sat in the lounger by the fireplace and welcomed the dog on his lap.

BoBo came in and plopped down next to Noah. "It's been a year, buds."

Jenny came over with a glass of wine. "Make room." She settled down beside Noah. "Might have been worse. We thought Mason was crazy when he when he started coughing and quarantined himself in his room."

Bobo threw a candy at Mason. "Hallelujah, you didn't get too sick or pass it to us."

"Noah's banana bread kept me going," Mason said.

"I told you, fairy dust is the magic ingredient!" Abby said.

"Fairy dust my ass. He sat outside Mason's door and kept him company for two weeks, made sure he kept up with school," Jenny said. "Not sure any of us would have made it without you."

"Thank god people around here masked up and took it seriously and kept the risk levels low. Can't believe the numbers in the Midwest," BoBo said. "Hey, Noah! I forgot to tell you,

I saw a bunch of people in your masks at the park the other day. That great African print."

The television showed scenes from Times Square. It was a different kind of crowd. Lots of people, all wearing masks, all keeping their distance.

"My sister in Manhattan tells me people there took it seriously. Now, the infection rate's low enough, they can get out some."

When the ball dropped, the cacophony was amazing, but the crowds didn't shout or sing. "Noisemakers don't spread the virus," the reporter said. The camera cut away to scenes across the city, people banging pots and waving flags from their balconies.

Ted got the champagne from the kitchen. "I'm tired and won't make it to midnight here, so let's raise a glass now."

BoBo passed glasses around as Ted poured. "Small glasses for the kids. They're part of this, too."

"To the new normal," Mason said.

Everyone raised their glasses and chimed in.

"The new normal?" Abby asked. "Shouldn't it be the new abnormal?"

Noah shifted a bit to settle further into the couch. "I like it," he said. "You know, the old normal sorta sucked."

Taking Possession

Nancy Sherer

Clarity Jones held the stack of hundred dollar bills in one hand and flipped through it. She shifted her weight from one foot to the other in a gentle dance while waiting to move up to the next red line. Funny, she thought, how things work out, when just two weeks earlier...

The threat was in blotchy red letters, Final Notice, stamped over Official Document: Do not delay. Clarity hadn't opened the other letters because, after all, they weren't addressed to her, but this one came with the sense of finality. Whatever was in this letter would affect her.

She slipped a steak knife into the corner to open it with a careful slit even though being neat wouldn't make a difference. Messing with mail was a felony. When she unfolded the paper, her eyes went straight to the all-caps line that demanded payment in full or the house would be sold for taxes. Where was she going to get that kind of money?

Clarity Jones was a twenty-three-year-old hair stylist, unemployed since the Orange Plague shut down the economy. She had lived, mostly alone, since Professor Spence disappeared. For all those six and a half years, the house had run smoothly on auto-pay accounts Spence had set up.

The kitchen was monochrome in the early morning light. She hadn't slept much the night before, but she was buzzing with nervous energy. She put a teabag in a cup of water, set it in the microwave, and pressed '2.' She squatted in front of a low cabinet, reached behind the frying pans, and pulled out the laptop that she had hidden there. She needed money, fast, and lots of it.

Roger Traut's body had been found washed up in the mill's treatment pond, but the sapphire jewelry known as the Star of Darling Downs he had stolen were still missing. Once she learned as much as she could about a suite of jewels, there might be a way to cash in. Treasure hunters might pay for supernatural advice. She had a good idea on how to make that happen.

Piper peered at her from the mudroom doorway. The bedraggled cat had been left behind when Professor Spence disappeared, but seemed determined to live until he returned. She stirred a raw egg into a dish of milk and set it on the floor. After adding milk and sugar to her tea, she sat down to research everything sapphire.

An hour later, she heard Jed get out of bed, and she slid the computer into a drawer.

Jed, a six-foot-tall, black haired, blue-eyed fisherman thumped down the stairs.

"Don't you have a clock in this damn place?"

Clarity glared at him until he mumbled an apology.

"There's a clock on the stove. It's almost seven. I suppose you're going to the waterfront to join the treasure hunt?"

"Nothing else to do. You wanna come? Maybe Baby Gaga will tell you where to look."

"Don't provoke Baba Yaga. She can be spiteful."

Jed finished buttoning his shirt, making an exaggerated stretch as he looked around.

"If you really believe that cr— stuff, why haven't you asked your ghost buddies to help with your money problems?"

"The money would be tainted by greed. I suppose I could give you a reading without offending the spirit realm. Maybe you can find the jewels."

"I can't afford you."

"Wait a second. Didn't you say you grew up around the dead guy? Rodney, Ricky…"

"Roger Traut. Lived on a farm a couple miles out of town. Sneaky little fuh… um…"

"Sneaky. Like how?"

"One time a bunch of mailboxes were trashed. Roger was right there the next morning hiring out to fix 'em."

She slipped out of her chair and gestured for Jed to follow her through the swinging oak door that separated the kitchen from the salon. "I'll give you a lover's discount on a Ouija reading."

Beyond the door, a mossy-green velvet drapery that she had salvaged from a theater renovation formed a wall. She flipped a light switch and pulled aside the folds to usher him into the room. A Tiffany-style lamp shade hung over a round table that was shrouded in a silky, white cloth made from a secondhand wedding dress, repurposed with smocking and embroidery.

Jed picked up a small iron statue of Leshi. Clarity grabbed it from his hand before pulling the tablecloth away to reveal a red table that was hand-painted with crude outline of animals, stars, and curlicues.

"Don't mess with things you don't understand. Just sit down while I get the board, and don't touch anything." She stepped behind the drapery and emerged with a cardboard game box and a candlestick. Sitting down across from Jed, she lit the candle and squared the board between them.

"Since you can only ask three questions, let's talk about what's important. Tell me what you remember about Traut and his family."

Twenty minutes later, Jed left through the kitchen door. Clarity slipped the wad of money that he had given her into her pocket, then tossed the sacred statue of Leshi from hand to hand. She might want a better-known guide to the Under-world. She'd give that some thought.

At ten o'clock Clarity wove her Cherry-crush red hair into braids, hung a wispy silk mask over her nose, and tied a pash-mina just below the waist of her jeans. She wiggled her hips, enjoying the soft rattle of jingle cones on the shawl's hem. As a last-minute thought, she tossed a deck of playing cards into her ditty bag. With a seductive glance to an imaginary audience, she walked out the kitchen door and headed for the waterfront through the odor of salt and seaweed blowing from the bay, random chirps and clucks of birds, the breeze rustling the leaves. Her financial problems were about to receive an other-worldly resolution.

She rounded the corner and turned onto the ROYGBIV overpass. The metal handrails were painted in rainbow colors.

She paused in the middle to look down across the parkway to the barricade where construction cones directed cars to a detour around the crime site. Traut's body had been washed up the day before. She hoped they hadn't found a second one. That would put a damper on the plan, but she would have to react to whatever chaos threw at her.

As she walked, she went over what Jed had told her about Traut. Sneaky. What else did she know about him? If Jed was half right, Traut might have pulled off the robbery on his own, but jewel theft was tricky. He was secretive. He vanished from school in seventh grade after his father was killed in a hunting accident. He claimed the Moonshiner's cabin as his own, keeping other kids from playing there. He took stupid dares to prove how tough he was. That was as much as she got before Jed insisted asking the first question for Ouija: Did Traut steal the jewels? Clarity swerved the planchette to a fast 'yes.'

She paused to check her reflection in door of the corner store. The windows of the mom and pop grocery were boarded up. It had closed over a year ago after the second wave of plague. Lots of empty buildings these days.

A masked dog walker nodded as he passed her at the intersection. A few businesses on the next block had survived. A pawn shop, a laundromat, and a used book store filled a strip mall. The scent of garlic and olive oil drifted in the air from the Italian restaurant on the corner. An employee with a red striped mask that matched her uniform was setting up for lunch service under umbrellaed tables.

At Bayview Park she followed a dirt shortcut down the hill. Two teenage boys with cheap, folding crab pots were watching the treatment pond on the other side of the road. They were both in shorts; a tall, freckled redhead with a backpack and a shorter boy with curly brown hair that stuck out from a baseball cap. Both wore bandanas as masks. Fourteen, she figured, judging by lanky bodies and just-broadening shoulders.

"What's going on?" she asked. "Did they find another body?"

"No, they have divers looking for the diamonds," brown hair said.

The redhead found his voice. "Not diamonds, there's a sapphire. It's the biggest one in the world"

When Clarity smiled at him, his face went red. "They think it's in the pond?"

"It's where they found the body," brown hair said, hoping for a smile like his friend got. Clarity obliged him, then went on toward the waterfront.

Across the road, a hodgepodge of buildings were piled at the bayside like contents of a giant junk drawer. Mounds of fishnets, tarp-wrapped speed boats, and stacks of commercial crab pots filled the boatyard. She scanned the bystanders wandering near the crime scene tape. Uniformed officers gathered in loose knots every few yards. Her lungs tightened, hard to breathe around so many rule-followers. Sun glinted off acrylic face shields except for one man who wore a black mask over his nose and mouth. Damn.

Detective Jesick was in street clothes, a short-sleeved blue shirt, charcoal-colored Chinos, and gray leather boat shoes. A pistol was holstered at his waist. Even when he was dressed like a used car salesman, he looked like a cowboy.

Clarity faced the two things she hated most, an authority figure and a man who didn't respond to her. But people respected Jesick. She had to do this, hold her act together with him, then other people would buy it. She straightened her back and raised her chin as she approached him.

"I have information." The words didn't come out as imperious as she'd meant them to.

Jesick glanced at her. "Take it to the station. They're compiling tips there."

"Traut didn't work alone." She watched his reaction. Did his pupils dilate? "There's a man, five foot ten, slender, you need to find him."

"Did you read that in a fortune cookie?"

Clarity could see people nearby were paying attention. She smiled behind her veil, making sure that it showed in her eyes.

"Pass that on. If anyone has questions, well, you know where my salon is." Her jingle cones rattled suggestively as she shifted her hips, turning to a wider circle of people. She put on her thousand-mile stare.

"He's still around. He hasn't left, but he's going to." She turned back to Jesick. "The Moonshiner's Cabin."

Someone in the crowd repeated her words accompanied by murmurs from others.

"What are you doing here?" Jesick said. "No cabins on the waterfront."

"I was drawn here."

"Draw yourself somewhere else. This is a murder investigation."

She was losing her audience. She raised her voice as though she was preaching in a church.

"The Star is near."

She would have had the crowd there if a cop behind Jesick hadn't tapped his elbow. The two exchanged information, then walked away leaving her prediction hanging in the air.

Jesick headed for the docks followed by a swirling current of people. A police line stopped them fifty feet from the boat launch. Gulls circled above before settling on pilings. News of a second body rippled through the air.

She remained in place as her plan dissolved. Fear replaced hope. It wasn't fair. A future of homelessness, hunger, dirt, and sickness lay before her. The crushed cardboard sign in her mind read 'desperate, anything helps.'

"I have a question." The man in coveralls shifted from one foot to the other. He was the one who responded to her moonshiner reference.

Clarity counted the seconds before responding. She touched her fingers to her temple. She hadn't planned the gesture, but she liked it and would keep it in mind for the future.

"The answer is 'yes.'"

"But you don't know what the question is."

"I don't need to know the question. The answer is yes."

"How much do I owe you?"

A uniformed officer interrupted them. "Panhandling is illegal."

"I don't panhandle. I accept donations for my church."

"So, you're a minister?"

"I am a Sybil."

Coveralls dug his wallet out of his back pocket and fumbled out a bill. Clarity ignored his hand, looking him in the eye.

"Many people will have the same question."

Coveralls opened his wallet again and pulled out more money. Clarity took it, and turned to the cop.

"I'll stop by the station with my Creed's Covenant. Until then, Blessed Be."

Clarity returned from the waterfront midafternoon and dumped the contents of her ditty bag on the kitchen table. She flattened the bills into stacks of fives, tens, and twenties. Seven-dollar bills came from a gaggle of teenagers. A skinny old lady handed her a twenty with a Blessed Be even though she hadn't asked for a reading. She counted and bundled $177 of folding money. She put the uncounted change—mostly quarters—into an empty pickle jar, then washed her hands. She needed to revise the plan. Handling money wasn't healthy. Maybe she would use a cloth grocery bag next time, have people drop the money directly into it, like a trick or treat bag. Another thing to give some thought to.

She dumped a can of soup into a bowl and put it in the microwave. She had stacks of Spence's mail, unopened except for that one. If his bank account was drained, she would have to start transferring bills into her name. Time for that if she got money for the property taxes. If she didn't, she'd lose it all just when she was so close.

She poured a spoonful of soup over a soda cracker and took a bite. She made more money in four hours than she would have gotten from two shifts worth of tips. Not that she would go back to work soon. Small-business beauty salons were plagued away. She needed to work the Sybil spiel.

Maybe she could work gloves into the act. No one was quite sure the plague was over, but everyone was going back to old habits, like hugs. Hugs were back. She'd had to twist out of several of them today, but the old Blessed Be lady caught her by surprise and made full body contact. More to think about.

She saw Jed coming around the side of the house. She scooped the bills into the drawer and spilled the coins out as though she was counting them.

"Clarity?"

"Let yourself in, I'm eating."

Jed came through the mudroom and slouched into the seat across from her.

"I went out to the Moonshiner's cabin today, but nothing was left. Like it sank into the swamp."

"Ouija said no. What's the point of asking if you don't listen?"

"I wasn't the only one out there. 'Bout noon couple dozen guys were tromping around."

As Jed went on talking, Clarity gazed intently at his blue eyes. Sapphire-blue, she realized. They were wide, and deep-set beneath thick black brows. His face was swarthy from life in the sun. She could see herself spending lots more time with him. The house was big enough, and it might be nice having someone else around. Her lips parted with an invitation.

"...catching crab... " Jed was onto another subject.

"You're going out on the boat? That sounds like fun."

"Nope. Work. Might make a thousand or even more."

"Can I go? What time are you leaving?"

"This is business, and it's bad luck to take a girl on a boat. But I can pick you up tomorrow night. Get some dinner. I'll stop by."

"That won't work. I have plans." She scooped the coins off the table back into the jar. "I hate to rush you out, but I have to get going." She got up, crossed the room, and opened the door while Jed was still trying to figure out what happened.

"So, we'll meet up at the bonfire tonight?"

"Like I said, I got something going. But good luck tomorrow."

She watched him follow the sidewalk to the front of the house, then stepped into the mudroom and hooked the lock and backed through the kitchen door. Like the oak door to the salon, this one had a solid lock. She twisted it shut and slid the chain down. She checked the windows, then went upstairs.

Her bedroom door was open, but the room was hot. She opened the northeast window, tossed the bedclothes back into place, then closed the door as she left. The other two bedroom doors were always closed. One room had an extra bed for company and the other she had taken over to store her junk, collected over the years that she had lived here alone. Well, almost alone, and almost all her junk. Eddie, her true love of three years before, had left behind his collection of Louis L'Amour and Executioner books. The used bookstore wouldn't take them, so there they were along with an assortment of stuff she picked up at secondhand stores in the days when she had a job. She pushed aside the box of masks, restacked some dishes, and pulled out the Hercules Home Vault. She twisted the knob and pulled the drawer open. She counted the money in the box. She added the day's take and counted everything again.

The key that dangled from the lock along with two others, the one that fit all the hundred-year-old locks in the house, she could try that one, last thing. She replaced the money, took the key, and re-hid the box.

She went downstairs, through the salon, to the walnut door that was almost black with age, to Professor Spence's room. Compared to opening his mail, which was a felony, invading his bedroom was creepy, but not exactly illegal. She opened the door.

Light filtered in from the drawn curtains. The air was quiet, thick with the odor of emptiness. She turned the light on to chase the shadows away. The walls, painted Artist White in the 1980s, were bare except for a wall clock that hung opposite his bed. A path was worn in the Berber carpet between the bed and the bathroom. The dresser was pushed against the wall next to the window, a nightstand with a lamp on it, nothing to distinguish it from a shabby motel room except for the medical equipment, a folded walker, a wheelchair, metal contraptions with mysterious functions, stacked in the corner, ready for future use.

A battered carry-on sat between the dresser and the door, just where she had last seen it. She went to the dresser. A yellow cardstock form meant to go to the post office with instructions to hold mail, travel documents, and plane tickets lay in a pile. Beside it, a money belt stuffed and ready to be strapped on. Taking the money would be larceny at the least, but more than that, an admission that she knew he was dead. She wasn't ready to do that.

She turned to leave the room, hesitated, then went to the closet. He had several tropical print shirts and a rack of neckties. She took a shirt and a necktie that was a Van Gogh's Starry Night print, then she left the room, pulling the door shut, and leaning on it before locking it.

Before leaving for the Dervish, she checked herself in bathroom mirror. The pink hibiscus with green palm fronds were just long enough to almost look like a decent length skirt. Underneath it was a white leotard. She added a belt at the waist while wondering if she should wear the suede buskins she found at the Salvation Army. The Starry Night, now with the seams ripped out, could be pulled up like a mask. At the last minute, she decided against the buskins—too costumey—and changed into sandals. Avant-garde, but not quite slutty. She thumbed a ride to the commercial district.

The nightclub, Dervish, was a former clothing outlet in a mostly deserted mall. The other stores had shut down during the first wave of the Orange Plague and never reopened. When the orange flags came down in January, Dervish emerged, first as a restaurant and lounge. Eventually management, a local Greek family, dimmed the lights, hired live bands, and turned up the volume. Now it was a hot spot for those lucky enough to still get a paycheck.

As Clarity walked across the parking lot, she rehearsed the backstory for the slightly worn pack of Vegas cards tucked in her ditty bag. Specific enough to be plausible—a disheartened real estate salesman winning big money in a Baccarat game—but vague enough to leave room for embellishment. She'd briefly considered scaring up a Tarot deck, but too many people played versions of that, and besides, it was cheesy. There was nothing spooky about crude drawings. A deck of playing cards had more possibilities. Add some obscure trivia about the pips adding up to 364, plus the joker for a full year, four suits—four seasons—and a few other things she would make up as she went and she had everyday magic.

The sun was still above the horizon when she pulled the door open. She waited for her eyes to adjust to the dim interior. Hulking shapes became stiff clusters of tables, and chairs sat in front of a vinyl bench that lined one wall. Shadows formed into people scattered among a dozen tables that edged a dance floor. Across the room, a raised platform for the band was equipped with speakers, mics and light boxes. Almost everyone had pulled their masks below their chins. There hadn't been a case of plague in Hamilton for two months, but the mask requirement had never been formally rescinded.

The door opened behind her, flooding the room with sunlight as people entered. Across the room a classmate from high school waved at her. The heart-shaped face framed in gelled, spiked blond hair with a button nose, and narrow, wide-set eyes wavered between being adorable like a doll and being freaky like a doll.

Lori was sitting with another woman and two men. Clarity waved back before going to the bar to order a drink.

"How much is a Coke?"

The bartender was a tall Black man who looked exactly like a football quarterback, which is what he would have been if sports hadn't shut down.

"Free to a designated driver," he said as he shoveled ice into a tumbler.

Clarity pulled down her mask and smiled at him

"Is it against the rules to put it in a regular hi-ball glass?"

"I make the rules." He met her eyes, almost winked, and reached behind him to a selection of glassware. He chose a tulip glass, tipped the Coke into it and dropped a cherry on top.

"What's your name?"

"Clarity."

"Then that's your order when you're ready for another." He leaned toward her as he handed it to her. He had out-flirted her, and he knew it. She mumbled a thanks that he might not have heard and went to join Lori.

"I'm Paul," said the man who rose to bring over a chair over from another table.

He looked old, maybe close to thirty. Good-looking, but tending towards pudgy. Nice hair with a conservative cut. His nails were neatly trimmed, his necktie was loosened but not off.

"This is Blayze," Lori indicated the other woman with a turn of her head, "and this is Craig."

Craig was angular, with broad shoulders and a nice profile, but his clothes had seen better days. He nodded at Clarity, then went on talking. Blayze leaned towards him, fascinated with the description of a new space movie that would be released in the fall.

Clarity checked out the people at other tables. Well dressed and coifed. Fifty bucks a reading was a real possibility.

"Where do you work?" Paul asked.

"She's a beautician," Lori said.

"That was BOP shut everything down." BOP meant Before Orange Plague. "I've been advising the police about the jewel theft. We found a second body, but no signal on the Star."

"Signal?"

Clarity gazed at the flickering light of the flameless candle.

"I'm a Sibyl, a conduit." She could sense Paul's skepticism because that would be how she would respond. "Detective

Jesick is focusing on the crime while I concentrate on locating the Star."

Craig paused his recount of the backstory of the soon to emerge superhero. "Second body?"

"It was an accomplice," Clarity said.

"I heard about that. The guy worked for the post office." Lori said.

The tables around them were filling up and the noise level was rising. A stray thought flitted through Clarity's mind. Before she could catch it, Craig started talking again.

"It came through Customs somehow. I don't think they carried it with them."

"If I wanted to get something like that across the border, I'd mix it in with junk jewelry," Blayze said. The mask that draped below her chin looked like a plaid beard.

"Too risky," Craig said. "He didn't steal the stuff without a way to move it."

The spooky mood that Clarity needed was dissipating.

"I'm going to talk to the insurance investigator tomorrow. I have to clear my head before then." Clarity shifted in her chair to reach her ditty bag that lay at her feet. "I have my cards with me, if anyone wants a reading."

"That would be fun," Blayze said. "Tell my fortune."

Craig tipped his head back and said, "Eenie meenie, chile beany, the spirits are about to speak."

"This isn't a game," Clarity whispered. "If it isn't taken seriously, it could turn bitter."

"Sorry," Craig said in a not really sorry tone. "Tell Blayze's fortune."

"Maybe. I usually ask fifty dollars for a reading, but since this started so facetiously, I might need sixty."

Craig shook his head slowly.

"I understand that some people can't afford it. And the future will happen anyway, so why not wait and find out? I should be focusing on finding the Star anyway."

Paul had been sitting back in his chair, holding a martini glass by its stem.

"He could have mailed it somewhere."

"The police would be watching for that," Craig said.

"Several of my clients set up post office boxes with the business names," Paul said.

Blayze had dropped her wallet back into her purse. Clarity didn't expect her to have the money. It would have to come from Craig.

"I'm going outside to watch the sunset." Clarity rose from her chair, took her glass, and smiled pleasantly before turning.

She stepped outside into the bright, early evening sunshine. A patio had been created using wrought-iron fencing that enclosed a half dozen tables. No one was sitting there now, but several people clustered thirty feet away sharing an ashtray. She chose a table farthest from the door, faced the horizon and sat down. She didn't check to see if anyone followed. She knew someone would come along, but she hoped it was Blayze and Craig. The cards were barely out of the pack before they came up behind her. She shuffled the cards while looking towards the horizon.

"Blayze wants her fortune told." Craig dropped three twenties in front of Clarity.

"I don't tell fortunes. I can interpret some things if the cards fall right." She glanced away from the bills that Craig put beside her drink. "Have a seat." She handed the deck to Blayze. "Cut the cards seven times and take one card from each pile."

Blayze's mouth was hidden, but her eyes were narrowed with suppressed, embarrassed interest. Clarity knew what she was going to tell her before she set the cards in three rows.

"There's a lot of luck here. When there is a question, things go your way. There is one sign that could be trouble, depending on the choice you make, but if you're careful it could bring you joy." She adjusted the cards, straightening the row, seeing Craig in her peripheral vision. He appeared to be a hard sell, but he had come up with sixty bucks, so maybe not. The reading was for Blayze, but he was the one she needed to impress.

She tapped on the jack of diamonds and looked into Blayze's eyes. "This might mean that you are about to have a great adventure, maybe travel somewhere unexpected." She moved her finger to the four of clubs. "You should say yes to new experiences." She let her hand hover over the cards for a minute. "Trust your feelings."

She scooped the cards up. "I hope that answered your question."

"What question?" Craig asked.

"That's up to her to reveal."

The sun was still well above the horizon, but rays bouncing off the bay reflected pink off the underside of the clouds. Clarity looked off in the distance as she tucked the cards back in the deck and cut them in long, slow motions. She had a feeling that Paul had said something important, something she needed to pay attention to. She could feel it darting through her mind, elusive, but still there. As Craig ushered Blayze away, a smooth faced man dropped money on top of what Craig had left. She pulled her mask over her mouth, smiled at him and handed him the deck.

It wasn't fully dark when Paul and Lori dropped Clarity off. She shook out the contents of the ditty bag on the table, sorted out the bills and a golden wedding band that she had taken in lieu of cash. Not enough money. Even if she could do four readings a day, it wouldn't be enough.

She paced out caffeine and anxiety by walking around the house. Finally, physically exhausted, she went to bed. Counting backwards by threes, she eventually she drifted off. It might have been an hour, it might have been three seconds, before she jumped out of bed.

That was what had been nagging at her all evening. Traut had rented a post office box. He could have used any name, but she wondered if she could guess it. Downstairs, at her computer, she researched variations of Moonshine, Moonshiner Inc., Moonshiner's Cabin, Moonshiner's Cabin LLC. Sometime after dawn, she found one with a local zip code. The post office box was listed under Moon's Shine. Before putting the computer away, she found out how much the insurance company would pay for the information.

Clarity walked up the county auditor's window with cash in hand for the taxes. It had taken her four hours on the computer to find a listing that contained Moonshine with a local zip code and a post office box. It had taken considerably longer, and the help of the insurance agent, to convince Detective Jesick to get a warrant for the mail contained in that post office box. Then it was a matter of days to receive the insurance company's finder's fee. After paying property taxes, she would have a couple thousand left over.

The clerk was a diminutive, pleasantly rounded, brunette. Her eyes squinted at the computer monitor.

"This address shows the property as belonging to Raphael Spence."

"Yes, he's unable to come here himself, and his electronic banking went wonky."

The tiny woman who was probably standing on a stool to see over the counter, peered at Clarity.

"Aren't you the one who figured out where the stolen jewels were?"

"A Ouija reading gave me a message from Traut's past. A walk with the dead led me to the post office. Finding the post office box registered to Moonshiner's Cabin was simple logic, but it was sort of spooky, even for me."

The clerk looked down at the money, up at Clarity, and didn't ask any more questions.

A Tale of Two Women in a Pandemic

Kim Bogren Owen

The Mother

She wished, for what felt like the millionth time, for him to stop moving. A tornado rushing through the house. Whirling here and there, toppling and building simultaneously, the sound of feet tapping and a voice answering its own questions. Until he stopped and looked to her for an answer—an answer to burning questions about how things fit, or to a rumbling stomach, or a broken toy. Motherhood could be exhausting.

Not that she saw her son as exhausting. She loved him of course, but the days did drag on. And fall was coming. Coming fast with more days of whirling, tumbling, stomping, always moving feet and voice. Days stuck inside with no end in sight.

Five minutes, she thought. I want five minutes for me. She remembered a story she had heard recently on NPR about education pods. Was that what they were calling it? Well, it didn't really matter, she realized. It would give her those five minutes and let someone else share their expertise. And she could share her expertise. What expertise did she have? Legal advice for five-year-olds? She'd read the parenting books, but still felt so lost as to how to parent. She'd always left education up to those who knew more about kids. Like Nanny. Now *she* was a gem.

It has been a stretch for them to hire her. Both she and her husband made decent money, but even so the $2000 a month was hard to swallow. It took over half her salary, making her wonder if it would be better if she stayed home. But she loved her job so she kept working and she knew if she took off a few years it would that much harder to find another job. She'd be behind in the work world by then. She put her laptop down on the coffee table in the family room.

"Want to come watch Wild Kratts?" *That would keep him quiet while she worked an*d did some research on these pods, as well as some real work. She was getting behind.

He came in, dragging his hand-knit fox behind him. It had been a gift from Nanny. Mother smiled at the sight of him. He was a mess with the blueberry yogurt from breakfast still covering his face and his hair jumbled as if clumps were each trying to escape his head in different directions. His bangs aimed for the ground partially obscuring his amber colored eyes. He curled up next to her and looked up at her. She brushed his bangs to the side and kissed him on the forehead. A haircut to free those eyes would have to wait until after the pandemic. He smiled at her. She relaxed deciding her research could wait and curled her arms around him forgetting about his Tasmanian devil ways for a few moments.

His partner in crime, a black lab named Gizmo, jumped up beside them.

"Gizmo and I made you into a sandwich. We're the bread and you're the peanut butter and jelly!" she said, laughing and turning the TV on for him.

He giggled, "I can't be two things. I'm just a tomato. That's my favorite sandwich. Tomato with nothing else."

He was sure to always be specific about his tastes. He had developed tastes of his own lately. About food, clothes, bath water temperature, bedtime… the list could go on. At times, it felt to her that it was all designed to test her resolve. She picked up her computer and typed in 'education pod.' A dozen links came up, which she opened and read. Feeling that she had enough of a handle on the subject, she emailed friends to see if they would want to be part of it.

Good Morning,

You all surviving another day in lockdown? We may get out for a bit of a hike later, but we'll see. I have a ton of work to get done and Nanny took the day off. I'm lost without her. I heard a story about education pods on NPR and it sounds like it could be a good thing. I really don't want to send him back to school if they open in-person and online didn't work for him. I know you all had similar experiences. An education pod might work best for us. We could each take a day to teach, focus on our strengths, and the kids could learn from each other. I see it as our own little school in the suburbs. Kind of like the one in Little House on the Prairie where different ages all learn together. LOL. We could even hire a teacher if we want. I think our nanny would be interested in helping out as an assistant. And we all have flexible enough jobs that we could swing a four day work week. Lord knows I would get more done if I had a day to myself. Yesterday, Noah knocked the plants off a table playing fighter pilot.

She closed her personal email and focused on responding to work emails. She had quit her job at a law firm when he was born so she could spend more time with him. When he was two she went back to work as legal counsel for a nonprofit that advocated for small farmers. She enjoyed the work. It gave her purpose outside of what she saw as her first purpose—being his mother. And it was flexible. On top of what her husband earned as an accountant at a big company, the pay let them live the life they wanted in the neighborhood they wanted. No fancy European vacations or designer clothing, but they didn't want that. A trip to Mexico to stay in an all-inclusive or Florida for Disney once a year, plus a few weekends to the coast, was enough. And since her preferred outfit was leggings, which the discount stores had in spades, she had what she wanted. A nice blazer over a pair of black leggings was all she needed most days for the office.

Throughout the rest of the day, she switched back and forth between her personal and work emails. When her husband got home, she told him about idea.

"An educational pod, huh? Interesting. My boss has his kid in one," he said.

"I think Noah would love it. He could get the attention he would have had at that private school we looked at and wished we could have afforded."

"The one that was more than my car?"

"Yes," she said. "It was nice. I loved the individual approach. He could have that."

"I think it's a great idea. I could take a day," he said.

"Really? You think they'd let you?"

"If there are twelve parents it would only be a couple days a month and I could work longer on the other days."

She hadn't expected that. He'd never been very involved with Noah's care. After the first couple of months of the pandemic, he was called back to work so he wasn't able to help much during the day. She often felt left alone to deal with everything while he was at work. Even though Nanny still came every day, Mother was the one who was responsible for making sure everything was taken care of. Bills, child care, meal planning, how to get out and still social distance, housework, appointments, the list went on. The pandemic hadn't changed that. It had always been that way. She kept the household and child schedules while he kept... his work schedule. He helped around the house as if he wasn't responsible for any of it other than to help her out. It left her often feeling frustrated. At least now he was ready to step in and take some responsibility for something. He would be her partner in this, and he would get to spend some time with Noah. This might change everything for them. Maybe he would realize what all went into running a household and caring for a child.

As they got ready for bed, she checked her computer one last time.

"All six families I emailed are interested. They're coming over on Saturday to talk about it more."

"Perfect. I'll make sure the lawn is mowed."

Case in point, she thought. He worried about how the lawn would look and missed what they would eat, where they would sit, who would watch the kids...

Early on Saturday morning, she ran to the store to pick up hummus, baby carrots, and pita bread. She had decided that everyone would be more comfortable with store-bought food rather than homemade. That was a sacrifice because she

enjoyed entertaining. That had been one of the hardest adjustments for her when the pandemic started. It was painful to not
have people over. She added a small plate of chocolate cookies
from a local bakery, as well as cups to go with the natural soda
for the children. There was wine and beer for the adults. They
spread lawn and camping chairs six feet apart in a circle around
the yard.

Noah stood on his oversized net swing and rocked it back
and forth. They had opted for the sixty inch one that could fit
several children on it. She told him he needed to wear a mask
when the other children were over. He had not argued. He was
just as excited as she was to see other people. As the guests
arrived, he took the kids straight outside to show them the
swing which had recently been purchased so they could all
swing and read stories together outside. The other children
were impressed with the swing, she noted, and smiled satisfac-
torily behind her mask. Life was good.

That night, as she climbed into bed and started to rub lo-
tion onto her legs, she went back over what happened at the
meeting. They divided the days of the week so they could each
check with their respective bosses. One of the mothers didn't
have flexibility with her job, but her husband could, and with
eleven adults in the rotation, it would work well. One mother,
Joyce, was on the fence if she was going to join. She said she
wanted to talk to her husband who couldn't attend. They decided to research curriculums that were open-ended and expe-
riential. One of the couples would do a forest school one day
using the forest behind their house and as well as taking the
kids on field trips to the beach and mountains. They had also
decided that Nanny could not bring her son to avoid him

distracting her from focusing on their children. Joyce disagreed pointing out they would have their own children with them, but she was overruled by the rest of the parents. They felt it was different when it was a paid job that needed to be kept the priority.

Mother pulled up her laptop and opened it to begin researching curriculums. The group decided to each bring back one or two ideas so they could decide next week. She wiggled in excitement. There was so much potential now for Noah. She could highlight his strengths and interests. He had spent a good deal of the time looking through the rocks alongside their house for the "shiny ones" with Nanny's son. *Maybe a geology curriculum would be fun.*

She thought about Nanny who had been at the meeting that afternoon to help watch the children while they talked. Nanny had to bring her son as she no one else to care for him. She had noted that Nanny made Noah his tomato sandwich after all the other kids. That bothered her. She knew it was silly, but still wondered how much worse it would be if Nanny's kid was always there.

"I'll let her know on Monday that we decided she can't bring her kid," she said half to herself.

Her husband nodded, "OK. I hope it doesn't become a problem. Isn't the kid starting kindergarten? What is she doing with him?"

She replied, "I don't know. I assume she's sending him to school. What other choice does she have?"

***

The Nanny

She pulled her hair back and swung her legs out of bed. She wished she didn't have to get out of bed and could stay curled up next to her husband and son. Her sweet boys. That's what she called them. Oh, well, Liam would be waking up soon and her husband would need to sleep late after his shift as a night watchman at the hospital. It was Saturday, and cartoons would be on, so Liam and she would normally be cuddled on the couch. Her arms wrapped around his little body and her face resting on his head. She loved his sweet smell. Would it go away as he got older? It had changed as he grew older.

Kindergarten. It was hard to believe he would be starting kindergarten this year and they were making the big choices that involved. They had opted for the neighborhood school rather than trying their luck in the open-enrollment lottery. They loved that he could walk when he got older and that his friends would be in the neighborhood. It felt odd to think about such things when only recently they'd been cheering him taking his first steps. They had been so excited when they found out she was pregnant. Life hadn't been easy for either of them, but his birth symbolized things getting better. More normal. They would live a normal life. Two parents, two kids, a picket fence.

It hadn't quite turned out like that though. One kid. No picket fence. At least not yet, but she was twenty-nine. Friends and family told her she had time. She wondered when it would happen. They were both in school and worked. She felt there was little time for other things, so these Saturday mornings were a special blessing where Liam could be her only focus.

But now she had to give it up. At least, they gave her overtime when she worked more than five days which always equaled more than forty hours despite an agreement to keep it to eight hours a day. She did her homework to complete her teaching degree when Mother took Noah outside to read a book or to eat together. She squeezed in time after she put the Liam to bed, as well.

She sighed. She wished that she had been born to a family with money. But then she looked at Liam snuggled on the bed. The ringlets of his hair encircling his angelic face. Oh, she wouldn't trade anything if it meant the possibility of not giving birth to him. People told her… no, they implied that if she'd waited they would be better off financially. She wondered if that were true. No one she knew with kids ever seemed to have enough money. Not even Mother and her husband always complained about how much they spent on Noah. Anyway, Nanny didn't have to give up the things she loved—her husband, Liam, and opportunities to get out camping and rock hounding. That was all the vacation they could afford now. Someday she hoped to be able to travel outside the country or to take Liam to Legoland. She tried to reassure herself with that thought. Though the upcoming start to school worried her. She didn't have time to go down this trap of memories and worry. She needed to get Liam up and out so they wouldn't be late.

She gently shook him awake. She had promised to go for a hot chocolate on the way over. A coffee would soften the blow for her, too. A rare splurge, but one she felt was well deserved. Not only was she giving up her Saturday, but she had already dealt with the Mother's frustration that she had to bring Liam with her. Mother worried it would take attention away from Noah, as if people never had two kids. It was so silly. The boys were only a year apart and played well together.

She handed him blue shorts and his favorite monster shirt. It had been handed down to him by Mother. He loved it. He stumbled into his room to get dressed as she took her clothes into the bathroom so she didn't wake her husband. She pulled on her jeans and put on a T-shirt with a flower button-down shirt over it. She went into the kitchen to grab two hard-boiled eggs and a couple of granola bars to eat in the car.

He walked in, shoes in one hand, and a knit aardvark she had made him. When he woke up, he was up. Like her. She smiled at him and took his hand into hers. He smiled back at her. His brown eyes lighting up the room for her.

"Ready to go, Mama?" he asked.

"Yes, sweetheart. Ready for hot chocolate?"

"I can't wait! Can we get a donut too?"

"I guess. If you eat your egg first. You need protein—not just sugar for breakfast. You did a great job getting up. We can go to the thrift shop afterwards to get you some new school clothes. Sound fun?"

Liam nodded. He was the rare kid who enjoyed shopping.

She held his hand as they walked down the cement stairs that led from their condo to the parking lot below. As she drove to Mother's house, her thoughts drifted back to him starting kindergarten. The district was planning on starting in person, but no formal decision had been made yet. She was very nervous about that. Their community had a lot of cases.

What if he had trouble breathing? He already had mild asthma. Luckily, his steroid treatments kept it at bay, but she worried it would become uncontrollable if he got sick. What would she do with work if he did get sick? Her husband could be home with Liam she guessed, but he would need to sleep. He was great and shared the household duties with her when his job and need for sleep didn't get in the way. They made a point of not leaving Liam alone with her husband while he slept.

Would Liam be safe? What if the school shut down or they needed to quarantine? What would she do then? Or what if they decided to do remote learning again? How would she work? She hoped if that was the case she could bring Liam with her.

She ran her fingers through her hair as her stomach cramped up in worry. Lately, this had been happening a lot when she thought about school for him. She wished she had more choices. Maybe she should have taken out loans. She would have finished school faster rather than on the slow plan of a course or two a semester and relying on grants and scholarships. Then she wouldn't have to be worrying about these things. Instead, she could be worrying about paying off her loans on a teacher's salary, she thought wryly. The what-ifs swirled around her brain creating a wall of fear and uncertainty, hiding everything else from her sight.

"Mama, that was the coffee shop!"

"I'm sorry! I'll turn around," she said as the wall fell and she became aware of what was around her. She pulled into a driveway and turned the car around. I can't let these thoughts paralyze me. We'll do the best we can. They pulled into the drive-through.

"Remember, Mama, you said I could have a hot chocolate and a donut! I ate my egg," he said leaning forward in his car seat and to show her the empty container.

"Good job. I won't forget my promises."

"But last week you said we could go to the park and then you didn't."

"You never forget a thing, do you? Except maybe when I ask you to pick up your toys."

"I get distratable."

"Distracted. Sometimes Mamas do too, but I won't forget this time and I'm very sorry I forgot about the park." They pulled up the intercom and she placed their order. Once they reached the window and got their order she looked at the time.

"That took a while! I need to drive fast."

"Don't get a ticket," Liam said. "That's what Dad always says."

She laughed, "I'll be careful. I have you to keep safe!"

It would all work out. It would all work out, she thought over and over. She pulled into the driveway at Mother's house. She wiped his face with a napkin before they got out of the car to make sure it was clean. She always felt that Mother gave her a side look when Liam wasn't perfectly clean. They walked up to the door and knocked on it.

Mother's husband opened the door, "Cutting it kind of close. Did the kid hold you up?" he said, rubbing her son's hair. She hated when people rubbed his head like that.

"No, he did great. We stopped for a treat and the drive-through was slow," she responded. "Don't you hate that?"

"Yeah, the shop by us is so slow. I can't go there before work."

"Ours is usually fast. I'm not sure what was up today."

"It's all good. I was just teasing you. Can you help in the kitchen? She's stressed out about the hummus and how to prevent sharing of germs," then looking at Liam, "Noah is outside on his swing."

Liam ran out to play with Noah eager to show him some fossils they had collected on a recent hike to a nearby waterfall, as well as the new Spiderman mask Nanny had made him. From the excited voices coming from the backyard, it seemed both were a hit.

She walked into the kitchen. Mother was running around opening hummus containers and putting cups of spoons handle side up into plastic cups next to them.

"Oh, you're here. Wash your hands. Then can you bring these out to the patio? I'm putting the spoons handle-side-up to help prevent them from getting contaminated. No sharing."

"That's a good idea," Nanny said as she washed her hands.

"I'm sorry, I just started ordering you around. I'm so stressed. I haven't entertained for so long. How are you?"

"We're fine. Nervous about school starting…"

"Me too! So nervous. Hopefully, today will help us find some resolution. Once you're done with that, can you help set up chairs, and then you can set up the Play-Doh Noah and I bought? They each get three colors and no sharing. Everyone will start arriving in about an hour." With that Mother zipped out the room to put the table runner on the glass table outside and then to find paper napkins.

As Nanny did what she was told, she wondered what Mother has meant by saying that today they could find some resolution. Was she going to be invited to not only work there but also be able to bring Liam? She had tried to bring it up when Mother asked earlier in the week about her watching the kids for their meeting, but Mother kept steering the conversation elsewhere. The conversation had been very frustrating and now she wondered if she dared to hope that Liam could join the rest.

After the parents were done talking about how they would set up the school, they spent an hour or so just chatting. It was lunchtime by then so the Nanny made all the children peanut butter and jelly sandwiches except for Noah. She made him a tomato sandwich. She also cut grapes in half. She didn't want any kids choking. As she was preparing the food, she noticed that one of the other mothers kept looking at her through the window. She thought her name was Joyce. Yes, that was it, Joyce. Her daughter often came over and played with Noah.

After lunch, Joyce came into the room and asked Nanny to help her out to the car. She had two older children and a baby so she said she could use the help carrying the baby's portable crib and car seat to her car. The Nanny started to pick up the crib, but Joyce handed her the baby.

"I can get those. You can get this little stinker," Joyce said picking up the other things. Once out the car she continued, "Jasmine, they aren't planning on letting you bring your son with you. I'm not comfortable with that. The great thing about pods is that it can help us break out of our boxes. Ironic, right, that a pod can help break a box? Anyway, I want more for my kids. I'm talking to another group of moms and I think they would be interested both in your working with us and in having your son join us. Would you be interested?"

"Yes, yes, I would," Nanny said as she remembered that as a child she had always played school with her three younger siblings. She always was the teacher. How she had loved that game. Now she might get to play it in real life before she received her degree.

"Liam loves rocks and geology. He was telling me all about them before we started the meeting. I'm guessing he gets that from you?"

"Me and my husband. We're amateur geologists."

"Perfect. I don't know a lot about it myself, but part of the whole pod experiment is each of us sharing our expertise and passions. I think you would bring a lot to the pod. Here's my number. Call me tomorrow after I've talked to the rest of the moms in our group. It'll be great to have one more Mother as part of our team."

Jasmine watched Joyce pull away as she put the card in her pocket and patted it. Who knew what other doors this could open or what direction it would put her life in? It looked like things would work out for them after all. As she drove away she imagined the look on Mother's face when she gave her the news.

GOOD VIBRATIONS

Bob Zaslow

He heard the hum first. Gradually, the twilight haze between deep sleep and surface awakening settled into place like the second-to-last piece of a jigsaw puzzle. Joseph blinked open his eyes. His first thought wasn't how long he'd been out, but what was that hum? His ventilator hummed, breathing in and out for him. Maybe that was it. But this hum... this hum felt omnipresent, like the virus. He even remembered hearing it while he lay in his ICU bed, unconscious.

Wait. He was unconscious. He couldn't have heard anything. In the next woozy minutes, Joseph closed his eyes and focused on being alive again. And the hum: *Can you be 'aware' of anything in a coma? Can you dream in a coma? Wasn't it just blackness?*

His body was in mechanical hands. Even his urine had been collected for him. But if he couldn't think, couldn't dream, wasn't sentient, what was that hum?

On some level beyond his ken, he sensed it was something new. This constant background droning, humming, created by no instrument or machine he had ever encountered.

Then, interest turned to fatigue and he tried to force himself to stop thinking about it.

That's just like me, he thought. Ungrateful to be pulled out of an eternal blackness and given back the gift of thinking: *So, be grateful. I'll see Anna soon. Where's the nurse? She's got to tell Anna I'm awake. Nah, don't worry about it and be happy to get on with my day. Get on with my day? That's funny.*

Joseph's day was more like a 24-hour cycle. His room was windowless. He had no way of knowing 12 AM from 12 PM until they returned his watch. His one constant was the hum.

Before the doctor and nurse undid his breathing apparatus and unplugged his ventilator, he guessed the hum would not disappear. He was right. This sound was something new, something beyond his understanding.

Until then, Joseph's left brain ran the vast majority of his understanding—ideas about other ideas, or ideas about ideas about ideas, in a kind of self-generated bureaucratic machine. Like countless images reflected in water with no substance.

He closed his eyes again and fell into a deep sleep. The hum became the sound track of a purple and yellow hummingbird flitting between purple clematis and yellow honeysuckle. But everything was slowed down to a thousand frames per second. Now, he could see each tiny feather in the hummingbird's soap-bubble wings. He saw himself watching from his wooden bench. As the hum grew louder, he took off from the bench and hovered over his yard, then his neighborhood. He felt like a single flake of white fluff in a snow globe.

Joseph relaxed into the sound of the hum and experienced it vibrating through his body and his mind and into his deepest emotions: *Nothing needs to change for me to be who I am. I already am who I really am. That's who is hearing the hum, that's what is alive in this moment and already allowing everything to be as it is.*

He awoke and saw with a new clarity that his true Self lets things be. A song flowed into his consciousness: *Row, row, row your boat / Gently down the stream...* Gently. Allowing, allowing, allowing. His ego, which has always worshiped winning, no longer occupied the boat. But this new rower says yes to everything in his experience. This yes is ongoing like the hum in the background. And now that he was certain it was not the ventilator's hum, he thought it may be some underlying subtle sense of an experience of a vibration: *Maybe this hum is the chord, the vibration of light. The energy of life.*

He turned slowly on his side and a new thought came to him: *Everything is energy. And energy is light.* Joseph continued to hear the hum as it became the vibration of light in his life, manifesting itself in his consciousness. A light far more subtle than the rays of the pinkest sunset.

After fifty-seven years and more than fifty hours in this room, he had never been more awake in his life. He remembered how many times he declared his vibrations small; how many times he watched his light dim. Now, he decided his is a light that brightens and dims depending on his state of mind. He also decided something bigger: *This light never blinks out.*

The nurse entered again and her eyes smiled behind her mask and face-shield. Her light was obvious to Joseph. He thought of all the times Anna's light should have been obvious to him, if he had only been tuned into it. He began to perceive a sense of universal connectedness. And now, for the first time in his memory, he saw his own vibration as a part of the world's.

Two weeks later, Anna helped him sit on his deck to look out at the water. His cat jumped onto the quilt on his lap and he watched her eyes close every time he stroked the top of her head. He knew she didn't have to be or do anything special to be loved. He listened to her purring—a constant low hum of joy—and when she fell asleep, he continued to hear the vibration he shared with her. And he made a choice to be awake and grateful. A choice born out of a second chance to continue on this enormous adventure.

DRIFT FOREVER

Van Peltekian

On the night before the return, Miriam Sarkissian was thinking about her family as the International Space Station passed over the United States. They would be passing over Burbank any second now. She'd wave down to them—her mom, dad, sister, her husband—and hoped they were all safe, wearing their masks, and were most importantly, healthy.

Mission Control assured them that they would be returning safely, but with the addendum that things will be different. That's what kept Miriam awake the nights leading up to the return—the notion of difference. When she had embarked on their journey back in October, Miriam (along with her colleagues Gregory Beatty and Hakim Abebe) had such a feeling of elation. After months of preparation and simulations, she was on her way into the unending frontier—outer space. She knew what to expect from the mission, but she'd still hoped deep down that there would be some kind of sci-fi wonderment to the experience. She didn't think that the sci-fi element of it would be taking place back on earth, however. Be careful what you wish for.

They had already been up for longer than planned. Three extra weeks, a consideration of their safety, Hidalgo at Control had told them through his facemask. They were extending it again for another three week stretch, pushing their tenure just past the eight month mark, further rattling the three scientists. *Will we be drifting forever?* She couldn't shake the nauseous fear at the prospect of another extension—and wouldn't the continued extensions just make their already weakened immune systems even more subject to the germ?

The germ. *The lead-in to a story of post-apocalyptia*, Miriam thought time and time again as she followed its rapid progress. They had first heard news of the germ around three months into their study.

"It'll just be another Swine Flu. Remember back in '10?" Gregory had said confidently when Hidalgo had first told them about it, and the potential for the germ's rapid transfer. "It won't amount to anything. Just media hype." The problem with Gregory, Miriam thought, was that while he exceled in his field, he seemed to know little outside of it, yet held onto a swaggering confidence, even though he might be wrong. Thankfully for Miriam, Control seemed to take little stock in his ambivalence and said to take caution and be weary. "It'll be gone before we know it." Gregory had said after the transmission.

As the days progressed into weeks, the crew watched in horrified disbelief as the germ spread from person to person, household to household, town to town, city to city, country to county. Leaping oceans and climbing mountains with ferocity, weakening the healthy and killing the weak. People were dying en masse. People they knew, people they didn't know. Miriam could almost feel it reaching up for her like an invisible hand, fingers brushing the exterior of the station as it made its rotations, leaving her with a knot in her stomach and anxiety-ridden night terrors. The germ had engulfed the world.

Tensions were rising from within the station as well. The unending drifting was getting to them all. Hidalgo had told them from the now almost empty Mission Control that there would be another extension. They found themselves arguing a lot, and their productivity dropping as fast as their morale.

Miriam worried constantly about her family. Even though she'd talk to them as often as possible, she couldn't help but worry this would be the last time she'd see any of them. Her mom and dad assured her that they were okay—they were working from home and leaving their house infrequently. Although they had a few scares due to interactions with people refusing to wear masks at the grocery store, they hadn't experienced anything negative. Miles, her husband, although furloughed from his job, remained in surprisingly high spirits, even with being alone for months in their two-bedroom apartment. Miriam was surprised when he introduced her to the two dogs he had rescued from the animal shelter, explaining that he needed companionship and hoped she wasn't upset. She was elated.

Miriam felt extremely fortunate, not just because her family was doing alright, but because she could be there for her crewmates as they needed her. She spent days comforting Hakim when he'd learned that his uncle and grandparents back in Ethiopia had all succumbed to the germ's unrelenting fury. Hakim tried his best to maintain his composure and focus as best he could, but every once and a while he would break down with worry, and Miriam would be there for him. They had formed a strong bond.

Gregory had spiraled into a downward depression after almost his entire family caught the germ at a reunion and a third of them had succumbed. He was listless, did little work, and when interacting with Hakim and Miriam, he was often spiteful and venomous. Miriam and Hakim tried to be there for him, but he pushed them away, and spent more and more time in his room, further isolating himself from their already extreme isolation.

"Happy Monthiversary," Miriam had said to Hakim one day while he was eating lunch, taking him completely off guard. He stared at her blankly.

"Excuse me?" he said.

"Eight months up here," she said. "We should celebrate." She wasn't sure if she was being genuine or cynical, but she felt like she wanted to say something to mark the time they'd spent drifting above the plagued planet below them.

"We will have cake," Hakim said. "When we return."

The return was what scared Miriam the most. While at times she felt the drift was unending, she knew she was safe from the germ. When they came back, however, and opened the hatch to the pod, the germ would be standing right outside, coming in without invitation. What would they be coming back to? Sure, they had been kept up to date on the state of things by Mission Control. They'd been sent a constant stream of information regarding how the world was faring form the impact of the germ, but experiencing it from arm's length through the news was different than being thrown headlong into it. She was plagued by recurring anxiety dreams of the crew landing on earth and finding they were the only people left. She wasn't ready to face that prospect. While she had kind of hoped deep down that they'd continue extending the mission and wait it out, she knew that that wouldn't be a possibility. At some point they would have to come out of hiding and face the beast.

Things would be different. It repeated in Maria's mind again as she sat amongst her peers as the descent began. *We're landing on an alien world.*

Despite the fact that down below all of Control was watching, making sure they would be safe. She knew that they would be coming to get them as soon as they landed, but she couldn't shake the nauseousness that gripped her and the unwavering prospect that the very people trying to rescue them could be carrying the germ. Her suit suddenly felt too tight, the air too thin. Get back to the station. They're leading us to our doom! It's not time yet. It's too soon. They're fools to go bring you back. Undo your belt and get back on the station. You can just drift. You can just drift forever. Wait it out! *Wait it out!*

Maria didn't remember the descent. She must have closed her eyes. Maybe she blacked out. Either way, when the fog in her brain evaporated and her vision made sense again, they were descending rapidly down, down, down, despite the parachutes—like the pod couldn't wait to get her back down to Earth and hand her over to the monster that consumed her nightmares.

Despite Hakim's assurances that she could breathe, she did her best to hold her breath, so as to not let the germ in. She held her breath for as long as she could before she sputtered and heaved in her first lungful of air on Earth since they'd left almost ten months ago for the mission.

She looked out the windows at the blue waters lapping at the vessel—it looked so familiar. The same sun beat down on them. The water was gentle, non-tumultuous, kind even in its welcome. The clouds were where they should be. Nothing abnormal. It was peaceful. It was beautiful—and yet, there was a weight in the air, and whether or not it was real, the weight in the air whispered caution.

The noise of motors broke her contemplation as the pod was surrounded, boats on either side. They had come, three motorboats coming to retrieve the pod, pluck it out of the water, and carry them all to the land. They stood sentinel-like as the boats ceased their roaring. All of them wearing masks that covered the bottom halves of their faces. All of them just eyes.

There was something about them that terrified her, and she turned away.

"Scared?" Gregory said. "You should be." She looked at him, at the hardened features, the pain he must be hiding, letting out as tongue lashings. "Welcome to hell." She held her head in her hands.

"Shut up," Hakim's voice broke through, solid, unwavering. He unbuckled from his seat and reached over, pulling her into him, holding her as they came closer. It was his turn to be there for Miriam as she broke down. "Hey, it's going to be okay."

"I'm frightened."

"We're all frightened."

Gregory opened his mouth as if to speak, but Hakim looked over at him and he quieted.

"I want to stay here. I want to drift forever on the ocean in the here where it's safe."

He smiled. "We can't do that. You know we can't do that."

They were being lifted onto the boat.

"It's all going to be so different."

"It will be different, but we will continue. We're all in this together. We will help each other." She looked at him, his smiling face and kind, soft eyes filled her with reassurance and comfort.

"You promise?"

"I promise."

She let her eyes land on the figures standing on the boat in their masks. They looked human enough. She wasn't in this alone. She wiped the tears misting her eyes and smiled back. "Okay."

The door to the pod opened. She inhaled deeply.

Welcome to the new normal.

TINY ERRORS

Tom Altreuter

Thinking things through has always been a problem for Nobel. He did better with collaborators who could point out various unintended consequences. He was a "Big Picture" type. Others were better at seeing the small stuff. Being of that super small subset of humans who could be called genius he had built the a time machine out of boredom during the quarantine.

He liked to travel and was an avid fan of history. Throwing himself into the project he stopped almost all contact with his staff. Deliveries piled up at his door, emails went unread and the phone was shut off to prevent distractions.

Deciding which way to travel was easy. The future just seemed like a bad idea given the outlook and the past looked like more fun. Having been tested and found negative prior to the lock down, he wasn't worried about dragging the plague along on his trip. Having lost track of the present time while he constructed his device, he started to look forward to getting out of the house.

The design of the device was a tip of the cap to Doctor Who and also a bit of a fuck you to Steve Jobs' sleek playthings. It looked like an exceptionally tall electric transformer box. Primer grey covered with various yellow "Caution" stickers he

had printed out. For fun he also sprayed on a few graffiti tags
to make it seem less out of place on the street. The tags really
made it seem ordinary.

Inside was also nothing fancy and nothing like a TARDIS.
It was a box with touchscreens, toggle switches and dials with
some LED lights on the ceiling. The platform he would stand
on was where the actual mechanism operated.

Nobel was excited to visit the past. So much had changed,
so quickly that he felt it would be interesting to see that time
with a fresh eye. The great disruption of the tech revolution
had upended and broken things with such efficacy that there
were bound to be some forgotten jewels to exploit. The idea
of some new venture to start had been bothering him for quite
some time. He was bored with his company and used to having
big ideas to play with. But now he was stuck at how everything
seemed to have been done. The thought of being left behind
nagged him.

Building the time machine had made his ennui apparent.
The device had no real commercial prospects. No matter what,
someone would find a way to use it to kill Hitler and then…
Nobel knew better than to try and change the past but using it
to jump start his present would be harmless.

For a test run he set the dial to 2001, the year he had
dropped out of school to launch his first company. He touched
the green start button. When he stepped out it was clear the
device worked. Pretty excellent but he somehow had ended up
in downtown Duluth during a February polar freeze. It was
June when he pressed the button, plus, Noble lived in the Pacific Northwest so that meant he had some flaw in temporal
adjustments. Probably something to do with the earth's

rotation. Figuring it a problem he could fix when he got back to 2020, he got back in to go home. It was blastingly cold outside and he was just wearing a T-shirt, jeans and sneakers.

He discovered his machine only went back in time. He discovered this when he stepped out into 1982 San Jose, California on an early spring day. Geographically and seasonally closer but still a little off. He had visited this city many times in his career but this looked nothing like the version he knew. He also wasn't sure why he had been dropped back another nineteen years. Something in the code probably.

Noble had been born in 1998, this dusty town of orchards was hard to believe as the hub of the future from where he had come from. He recognized the city only because of its downtown cathedral, which, like the rest of his surroundings, looked about to fall down from neglect. He realized he was in trouble. The device sat on a corner looking like it had always been there. He looked around trying to find a cab, no UBER, what a world. The neighborhood looked like the type of place no cabbie would willingly roam. With no better option he trudged to the freeway and put out a thumb, hoping to get to Palo Alto where help might be found. His phone was, of course, useless, battery was low and he had forgot his charger. It was hours before he caught a ride.

"So, where ya going?" His Savior was a button down type, wearing a tie with a short brush cut hair. The Reagan/Bush bumper sticker showed at least the chronometer is functioning properly.

"I need to get to Stanford. Thanks for giving me a lift, really appreciate it."

"Stanford huh? You a student?"

"Was. Left to put together my first start up. Now I just drop by for panels and stuff mostly." The dude doesn't know his celebrated (by some) rider. Noble enjoys the obscurity. He almost feels safe.

"Start up?" The drivers tone suggests an unfamiliarity with the term which Nobel is quick to realize is not in the current vernacular of this time.

"My own company…" Noble can see the guy is skeptical. He's somewhere around forty, probably a realtor. Drives a BMW though and has one of those laughable shoe box type phones tucked between the seats. "Umm, like coding. Computer stuff, for like games."

The driver snorts. "Mean like at the arcades? OK kid, good on you. Hope it works out."

Nobel thanks him and they just ride in silence for a while. The radio is tuned to a Giant's game but the ads are what capture Noble. Most of what is pitched no longer exists.

"Look, I don't pick up hitch hikers normally but I gotta ask about the shirt. What the holy fucking hell does it mean?"

Looking down Nobel see's he is wearing his "Black Lives Matter" T. He had bought a bunch back in May when his public image had been getting some hard hits about his disassociation from politics and what his platform allowed as content. Nobel has been wearing them without any thought but for PR, but a thunder clap sounded in his head and perhaps dressing more neutral would have been a better choice for time travel. The driver lights a cigarette and that's the smell Noble has been trying to locate in his memory when he first got in the car. He cracks his window and tries to come up with an answer.

"Gamer code talk, like glitches in the code where you need to patch fixes but those matter because even though they got overlooked they're like almost more valuable than what the code was written for." There is no way to explain to the driver the context of the shirt. Eighth inning, Giants down 14 to 1 and the driver punches the keys on the analog console cursing at the team to himself. "What a Fool Believes" floods in about mid chorus.

Driver lets Nobel out in downtown Palo Alto. Tells Nobel to stay away from the east side of town. Noble tells him to buy stock in Apple computers and to hold on to it no matter what as a thank you.

He heads toward the Stanford campus, the offices of the physics department as his goal. As he walked he notices strange things from old pictures. The dromedary humps of blue and brown mail boxes, pay phones and a lack of ATMs along the streets while homing in on the familiar spire rising over the grove of trees that was his true north at the moment. Restaurant names and buildings in this now (looking like a then more and more) that seem hard to imagine ever existing. Everyone seems to be smoking cigarettes.

The whole thing would be like being in a movie except Nobel is starting to get a bit freaked out. Shipwrecked becomes a frantic mantra and his pace quickens. The soles of his Jordans (limited edition—2003, gift from his dad, worn in his memory and honor) slap along the pavement in rhythm with the urgency of the thought that he hasn't even been born yet and can't remember his mother's maiden name for a security answer.

Always been a sneering dick about others being not ready for a coming shit storm. In the future he has a private retreat in New Zealand. At the moment he's weaving past crack dealers, pimps and the other types of disposed humans he has never had to acknowledge. He could be in his time but this is his first experience on the street with no driver or GPS in over a decade.

Nobel had assumed he would be back before lunch and the smell of food reminds him that he only has had a protein bar and a beet, oat, kale, almond smoothie for breakfast. He has some folding cash in his wallet which he usually uses as a show prop of generosity for journalists. Pulling out a C for the guy with the cardboard sign outside the restaurant, that sort of thing. His brain needs fuel to think. The experience has been far more arduous than as originally conceived.

Picks a place that has table cloths and servers. A nice glass of wine would help settle his nerves and is likely to be far more hygienic than any of the student dives he has passed. The restaurant's interior is dark, everything is muted colors. It feels like a library to Nobel down to the bulky board like menus bound in faux leather. Super old school. It actually tickles his senses. Perhaps this would be a fun dinosaur to revive. Be kind of cool to own a restaurant like this, all the retro vibes are begging to make a comeback in his real time.

He is refused a table. Apparently there is a dress code. Jacket and tie rules. Nobel imagines the possibilities. The Matire D', sneering at his T-shirt, asked for ID and when presented with such walked Noble outside and let him know as far as fake IDs go, Noble had been ripped off. Once again the T-shirt came up. Matire De asking him if it is a band. Noble tells him it's a band and slogs away towards some golden arches a few blocks up which accept money without regards to appearances in any timeline.

What was trouble with some sort of possible good outcome got skewed upon later reflection. Nobel had not been inside a McDonalds for years. It is a far more contained atmosphere in this now. Drinks are not self-serve for one thing and it may just be this place but everything appears dingy and drab. He only looks at the menu board to see what's not there. Very few pictures of items for offer. Just a list and the suggestion of a value meal is present but the most space is reserved for the kids meal. He goes with a Big Mac, a Coke and fries. He takes out a hundred, no card readers on the counter, and apologizes for the fact that he is only carrying large bills. The fact that the meal is going to be well under six bucks makes the denomination proffered seem disproportionate overkill. Nobel sees the kid's eyes pop but chalks it up to it being maybe the first time this kid has ever seen anything larger than a twenty. Kid says he need to get the manager.

The manager comes over and examines the bill while giving Noble a once over twice. Guy looks about his age, Noble wonders about what ever happened to this guy? Did he get his shit together? Nobel makes a mental note of his name tag, Calvin A Hoobes, and is going to google it when he gets back. Calvin whispers something to the kid, who now seems nervous. Whatever. The change is exchanged and Noble takes a seat while waiting for his number to be called. He sits by a window in order to fully enjoy the fashions of 1982 in real time passing by.

The food seems frozen in their own continuum. They taste and look the same as he remembers, as if time had somehow been evaded. A couple of cop cars pull up and park. Perhaps lunch and a show? Lights aren't flashing so they are probably here for the same reason he is, lunch. He looks at his watch but since it's tied to his non-functioning phone, it too, is a brick.

As the cops head to the counter Nobel loses interest and goes back to swiping small bundles of fries through the pools of catsup he's squeezed out of packets onto his entrees wrapper. Decides that before he leaves this era he's going to see how much mint vintage retail he can bring back. He smiles at the thought.

Instead, he finds himself arrested. He demands to know the charges but the cops just read him his rights as they cuff him. Soon he is booked at the station house, relieved of all personal items down to his shoe laces (a few comments about his Jordans get exchanged, Jordans not being a noun yet) and placed in a room, cuffed to a table. He knows what this room is, that the mirror is a two-way. What he wants to know is why? He has broken no laws except maybe one from the books of temporal physics but no one here would know or even understand that.

A detective walks in. Nobel knows he's a detective because the guy just screams trope in his dress and manner. Introduces himself as Detective Nosserall, sits down and goes silent. Obviously the guy is thinking he's some expert on brinkmanship just sitting across the table from Nobel and staring. Also, obviously, he has no idea that the guy he is staring down has played this game with giants such as Zuckerberg and Musk (although never chained to a table). Noble just wants to go home. He asks why he is being held and what the charges are.

The detective sighs, extends his arms with his fingers interlaced palms out, facing Noble and cracks his knuckles before resting his arms on the table. Noble notices the lack of paperwork, not a pad or a pen in sight. Decides, right then to lawyer up. Lieutenant Nosserall informs Noble (in a tone that hits heavy on air quotes about the name as being believable) that there is reasonable suspicion that he has been passing counterfeit bills and that he is only being held until the treasury department sends someone over. Asks about the shirt. Nobel says it's a band. He then leaves and Noble remains confined and locked to a table regretting the fact he had ordered a large drink earlier.

The Feds arrive. Four of them. Two treasury, two FBI. Noble really needs to pee and says as much. He gets cuffed hands front and shackles ring his ankles so he can shuffle down the hall with two guards, one on each side, to escort him to the bathroom. Once relived it's back again with the room full of black suits who seemed to be fighting over who has jurisdiction. Nobel tells them he wants his lawyer present before he will say another word. His team will eviscerate this cheap suit clown squad in a matter of minutes. Tells them to contact Psych, Curry and Crash and savors the discomfort on their faces at the name drop. Even fifty years ago the firm was known as nothing to be fucked with and one of the feds signals to someone behind the mirror to make the call. Nobel smirks. He lives for seizing the advantage.

Unfortunately, the retainer Nobel pays is not retro-active. They have never heard of him or his company. Ransom Curry, his personal lawyer, like himself, has yet to be born. One of the agents opens a briefcase and begins placing Nobles pockets contents on the table. First question is about the shirt. Nobel wonders if he should have brought a carton of them to sell since everybody seems interested. Says it's a band.

They want to know about the phone. They don't know it's a phone because it is not one in their visual reference, same with the watch. Nobel figures out pretty fast who is FBI and who is treasury because the money guys are super interested in just what Nobel was up to trying to pass, such blatantly over-wrought forgeries, so much attention to detail while still screaming "fake". FBI are focused on his devices and his driver's license. The treasury guys are also fascinated by that item due to the elaborate time involved in producing something very different from a forgery. Both have questions about Russia and Nobel is glad he isn't carrying a passport because last year he was there on business five times. They keep saying USSR so what he hears is yousserr and has to ask if they mean Russia because the way they say the acronym makes Noble think of the way you pretend cough a word behind your hand as a joke. They don't seem to be joking.

Nobel goes with the gambit, knowing well just how thin the ice might be, to start with the truth. He understands the risk. Any disclosed information about the future will alter it but they have a table full of such so he gives it his best evasive answers while trying to persuade them to just get him to the labs at Stanford where he might be able to clear a few things up about everything which might be hard to explain on his own.

Alpha FBI asks again about the shirt. Nobel explains the meaning, trying not to cite specific future events, just the idea of a system that is heading into becoming so lacking in justice that equality and democracy are heading off a cliff. The suits are not pleased. They stand and depart after gathering back the items marked and numbered in zip lock bags. An hour or so later he is led, shackled, hands behind his back this time to a black van.

He is transferred to a plane from the van and after several hours in the air he is to be placed in another black van. He is standing in some flat, arid place, on the tarmac waiting to be loaded. Still chained. He left no notes in the future. No one there will know where he's gone. The white board in his work shop would offer only equations a genius like him could decipher. Only meant to step out for a minute.

Nobel, begins to understand this is now his time. His future, the place he left is now his past and the confinement he sought to escape has been shrunken to a six by ten cell somewhere in Colorado. Monthly evaluations from specialists representing various fields come to talk to him and ask questions. They are the only contact with the outside and all give him no news about the state of the world. Nobel gives up nothing in return. He can only wonder the damage he has done from just being bored.

MASQUERADE

David Beaumier

The last two and half years have given him the covid twenty and then some, so he goes thrift shopping one week before his community's first tango social post-quarantine. He brings his own clothes that no longer fit him, carefully culled from the very stores he now browses, to exchange for credit. The musk of second-hand clothing permeates his mask. Maybe one in four of the other customers also wear face coverings, which makes sense since both the national and state mandates have long since been lifted. Now most people wear them only when they feel sick, but he likes to be more cautious, and he suspects other people do, too. Keeping six feet away from others is also a new polite habit, even though the signs encouraging it have been taken down.

Every pair of dress pants that might fit winds up in his arms. He carries them over to the fitting room, marveling that he can use a fitting room. He's pleased to see that the employee at the counter wears a mask. He deposits the pants, tamping down his eagerness to try them on now. Instead, he squeezes a pump of hand sanitizer over his palms, and then forays back to the racks to pick out dress shirts. Dark colors are a favorite.

Friends always say he's too pale for pastels, and after all that time, bleached even whiter by screens, he's not ready for anything that would even hint at him being washed out after so much time indoors.

It feels like an accomplishment to have finally gone from a small to a medium, having been underweight for so much of his life. He still remembers when he was little he was taken to a nutritionist who asked him to describe how much peanut butter his parents generally put on his sandwiches. At the time he felt ashamed, like he was bad for being a picky eater, and he didn't understand why they were concerned. Twenty years and one pandemic later, all those home cooked meals and pints of ice cream to reward him for keeping up his tango drills, not to mention the many six packs of beer to help the days pass, had added up to make him look positively filled out. Looking at the tight-fitting undershirt he wore to test these clothes out, he realizes that it, too, will need to be replaced. Three basic Hanes shirts answer his call, all placed in slightly different areas along the shirt rack instead of grouped together as one might expect.

At the end, he has three new pairs of dress pants, two white undershirts, a black undershirt, and four new button ups, the prize of which is a dark forest green. He always dreamed of finding a green shirt like this ever since an old dance partner said he'd look good in this color, and it felt like kismet to have found it at this time.

Better late than never, he supposes.

The next order of business is a haircut. Six months in, barbers had reopened. But what was the point of putting himself and others at risk when no one would be close enough to see if his hair was a little uneven. He couldn't stand that awkward phase where hair started growing over his ears, so he just went into his backyard and cut his hair there. He was surprised that all of the videos he could find online for men's home haircuts just talked about using electric clippers, which was a little bit too close of a shave for him. Still, his hair looked good enough in all the video calls that stood in for normal human connection. Now that people will see him in person, he feels nervous elation to be going back to his favorite barber, not sure what it will be like to sit still indoors for so long.

He writes his name on a clipboard, and almost no time passes before he's called. The touch of the stylist causes an involuntary flinch. He wills himself to be still, force his muscles to relax.

"First haircut since quarantine?" she asks, her voice gentle.

He asks if it's that obvious.

"That's alright, honey, we'll have you all cleaned up in no time." She taps the strings that secure her own mask to her face. "This'll need to come off." She's wearing a mask, so that should be okay, but still, they're inside. He knows he can't expect her to cut around the mask, so he takes it off, wondering if his smile still looks natural.

"That's better." She's so at ease as she moves around him, her fingers combing through the uneven strands of his hair and bringing it all closer to his temples. He feels muscles that he didn't realize had seized up start to relax at this human touch. His hair is still short, so it doesn't take long. It's disappointing when the blow dryer comes out, but the feeling of loose hair blowing off of him leaves him feeling strangely clean. She ruffles his hair when done, and he blinks several times before he's sure he won't cry.

He knows he tips more than is customary, but he can't help it any more than the smile that's glued to his face as he puts his mask back on. He forgot how itchy it is to get a haircut, and when he gets home all his clothes go in the wash and he goes in the shower.

The week slides by until it's time. The day has arrived. It used to be he would show up an hour late to dance, but today he eats an early dinner because nothing in the world will stop him from enjoying every second of this social. First, he puts on a playlist, letting the dance music flow through the room. While he dresses, he can't help but think of Hera in the *Iliad* as she dresses to distract Zeus from the Trojan War. This outfit won't determine the fates of countries and lives, but still, his fingers tremble as he carefully buttons his forest green shirt, feeling the clean material on his wrists. It has something that firms the cotton, and the slight raised ridges will give him a nice flowing look as he dances.

He used to tell employers that if his schedule ever interfered with his dance schedule he would quit. It was all that kept him sane, and now he wasn't sure if he had exaggerated or not. How much of the last two and a half years without dance did he just try and pretend he did not exist? How many hours did he imagine floating in a void where nothing could touch him, and, for those hours in the dark, he didn't need to worry or feel afraid about the world falling apart outside.

The reverie and ritual of the dance brings him flooding back to the present when he automatically sprays cologne into the air and walks through it. Even this small amount feels like too much after years with no artificial scents outside of the shower. Memories flood into him as the music swells. Buenos Aires, stepping out to smoke with the followers he came with, the only time they allowed themselves to talk. The feeling of a partner's hair drowning the right side of his face as stranger after stranger pressed against his cheek.

Ready, he checks himself in the mirror, dark eyes visible over the green mask that matches his shirt. He wishes he had a matching pocket square, but that could be for the next event. During quarantine, his talent for gauging online clothes had grown beyond what he had imagined was possible. He runs his hands over his stomach. His extra weight would make dancing different, but he feels prepared after so many nights dancing in his kitchen, holding a chair in front of him as his stand-in partner. Once, an older guy built like a snowman gave him advice. "You can spend decades practicing your embrace." The man slapped his belly, making it jiggle. "Or eat well and the result is the same! No one dances as well as a fat man."

He does a little hop. Not quite fat, but definitely filled out. Smiling at the thought that maybe he's one step closer to that perfect tango embrace, he grabs his shoe bag and hops in his car. It's strange not to be driving to the grocery store, but instead to a social event with real people. The dance studio is nearby, but he's refusing to lose any time or to show up tired or the slightest bit sweaty from walking. He keeps the music playing on the stereo for the drive, despite the short distance, and Juan D'Arienzo's "Cicatrices" plays over the stereo.

"*Cicatrices, incurables de una herida que me ha causada la vida en su triste batalla…*" He glances at the screen at a stoplight to check who the singer is. Héctor Mauré. He should have remembered that, and he tries to remember other singers, but only Alberto Castillo comes to mind because the man ran his own orchestra. Of course that was after Castillo stopped being a gynecologist at his wife's request. Something about his practice becoming too popular after people discovered he was a famous tango singer.

He arrives at the dance hall before the song even ends. No wonder he usually walked—it's so close. As he parks, he leaves the car running so that Mauré may sing the last notes. "*Cicatrices de mi vida que aunque no tienen encanto, yo las quiero tanto y tanto que jamás, jamás ya nunca olvideré.*" He wonders, as he slings his shoe bag over his shoulder, if the scars of everything will be worth remembering. Worth the pain and the waiting.

Inside, the room is lit up, more early arrivals than normal sit and a few couples dance, yet conversations are muted. He pays. The woman at the ever-present money table crinkles her eyes behind her mask. It's as if this isn't the first tango event in too long. Despite phase four relaxing all restrictions just over two months ago, everyone is still careful. So many communities tried to come back too soon and suffered for it just a year in. His own community had already lost so much of the older crowd to cancer that they weren't willing to test the pandemic, and he was grateful. The world already felt suffused with much death and sorrow.

Plenty of people had traveled from cities a couple hours north and south from here for this event, which shouldn't surprise him. Still, it feels strange to see so many unfamiliar faces at what somehow still feels like the local dance he has always attended. He sits down at the table that he usually takes, and pulls out a flask and a bottle of hand sanitizing spray from his shoe bag and sets them both in easy reach.

Then he puts on his shoes.

He's worn them time and time again on his tiled kitchen floor, but they belong here on hardwood. He ignores the flask for now, not wanting to deal with the mask on, mask off struggle, and instead watches the dancers. They always dance for three to four songs until the *cortina*, a song that is not tango, plays and signals the appropriate time to say thank you to your partner and return to your seat. This next *cortina* is a sample of Leonard Cohen's "Hallelujah."

As soon as the steady thrum of the double bass starts up, he raises his eyes and searches for a partner. His gaze settles on a gray-haired woman, maybe twenty years older than him, comparable in height, and wearing a simple blue dress and a sunflower mask. He likes the confidence of her posture. Seeing her wearing a mask told him she wasn't chatting, but ready to dance. He hopes his mask tells her the same.

She meets his eyes.

A rich voice fills the room as he nods to her.

She maintains the eye contact, and he spritzes his hands, the familiar alcohol burning in contrast to his cologne, before quickly crossing the room as other people complete the same ritual, their own dances quietly arranged.

It all feels strange and new. He walks within six feet of her, then holds out a hand. "Would you like to dance?" already knowing the answer.

"I would." She takes his hand. Glancing behind him to make sure no one is already speeding down the line of dance, he leads her just onto the floor, and raises their hands, his left and her right, up to their shared shoulder height. He holds open his right arm. She steps in, her left arm encircling his shoulders until they are pressed chest to chest. He feels her soften into his stomach, and only then does he close the embrace, his right hand resting on her left shoulder blade. Together, they breathe deeply.

And they begin to dance.

A WALK IN THE DESERT

Raj Gill

San Francisco New Year's Eve revelers twirled noisemakers below David Drummond's office window. Drivers, forced to wait in a line of cars on Battery and Pine, also joined in the festivities, honking with glee and enthusiasm instead of their usual rage and hate. David pressed his cheek against the glass, peered down, and let out an exasperated sigh. "People, it's just another day. New Year's occurs at least once a month depending on what country you're standing in."

He squinted as he scanned the street. Men and women in power uniforms and Italian shoes marched beneath tilted umbrellas organized in a Roman tortoise formation. A few broke ranks to spin noise makers or shoot confetti poppers that rained back down on the tops of the umbrellas. He traced the line as far back as he could see—the heart of the financial district.

Between the seams of the umbrella canopy, he saw a man with his mobile pressed against his ear. David tracked his movements. The man seemed to glide on the sidewalk, his broad shoulders filled his fitted navy trench coat. David shifted in his seat, briefly catching his own drab reflection in the mirror. He peered once again and imagined himself walking with confidence wearing the man's designer clothes. He wondered where his evening would take him: on his way home or to a bar? When there, would he be joined by his family or friends? And who would kiss him at midnight? David recalled the bittersweet memory of his ex-fiancé kissing him at midnight three New Year's Eve's ago. *I wish I'd known that was the last time I'd feel loved.*

The metal end piece of David's glasses scraped against the window and brought him back in the moment. He leaned in to get a better view of a woman that caught his eye across the street. Standing at the edge of the sidewalk, wearing a pair of novelty glasses and an oversized beaded necklace, she waved her hand, trying to get the attention of the taxi boxed in the center lane. She craned her neck towards the second story office window and stared back at David through glasses with oversized zeros that framed her eyes.

"Double D!" Joe pounded a fist against David's desk.

Startled, David banged his head against the window, leaving an imprint of oil in the shape of his forehead on the glass. He glanced down and saw the woman flipping him off.

"You sly dog, who are you staring at today? Blonde or brunette?"

"None—I mean no one. Just, heard a noise."

"It's quittin' time Double D! People just excited about being done with this god forsaken year." Joe thrusted his hips forward, raised his hands in the air and hollered, "Bring on 2020!" Joe wiped spit off his lips with the back of his thumb, "Got any plans tonight, Double D?"

"No. No plans. It's just another day. Actually an interesting fact, New Year's is celebrated about every month depending on—"

"Yeah, I booked a table at the missus' favorite restaurant, and I sent the kids to stay over at their grandparents in Petaluma... so it's going to be a great start to the new year." Joe winked.

David distracted himself from the conversation by cleaning his glasses with his pocket handkerchief. "That sounds... good, Joe."

"So, you're not going out?" Joe picked up a framed picture of the Golden Gate Bridge perched beside the computer monitor on David's otherwise unadorned desk and inspected it. "Don't you have any friends? Family? A girlfriend? ...A boyfriend?" Joe tossed the frame onto the mouse pad.

"No, no, no. My family is scattered across the country. And... I just prefer being alone."

"Hell, do you have a pet? Everyone's gotta have someone?"

"Can't afford the pet rent and vet bills."

"Well shit, you gotta get out there, kemosabe. Play the field, get yourself a lady... or a man, hey..." Joe threw his arms into the air, "no judgment from me."

"Really Joe, I'm good. I just prefer being alone."

"Suit yourself. Different strokes for different folks, I guess. Well, I'm gonna head out. I'll catch you..." Joe shot finger guns at David, "next year, Double D!"

"Have a good one, Joe." David waited until his colleague entered the hall. He retrieved a disinfectant wipe from his desk and cleaned the frame before setting it back in place. He continued working until the last person in the office left for the evening. He shut down his computer and watched the monitor fade until only his reflection remained on the black screen. *Where did it go wrong?* He asked the man staring back at him. *When did fated circumstance become preference?* David spent a minute cycling through the myriad of excuses he's used to convince himself that being alone since his break up was better than the alternative. But the counterargument to his loneliness—the vacant hole yet to be filled in his heart—was the constant thrum that he inadvertently tuned his life to.

He checked his mobile—no emails, texts, missed calls, or social media notifications. After setting his phone on the desk, he slipped his canvas jacket onto his shoulders and wrestled with fitting the hood over his head. After checking his phone one last time, he switched it out for a book in his satchel and embarked on his two hour commute out of the city to his studio apartment in Richmond.

"First it was the fires down under, then Kobe's death, and now…" Joe pointed to his face mask, "…panties on your face?" What's this world coming to? I thought this year was supposed to be different?"

David nudged the bottle of hand sanitizer on his desk closer to Joe.

Joe seemed not to notice or care. "And why are we even here? If it's so bat shit crazy we have to hoard tee-pee and quarantine in a bunker, what are we doing standing in the middle of downtown San Francisco?"

David pumped sanitizer onto his own palm, then embellished the movements of his hand cleaning ritual hoping to entice Joe to do the same.

Joe ignored him. "And these masks? I can barely breathe with 'em on." He lowered his cotton face mask onto his neck.

David lurched back in his chair, distancing himself from the man standing beside his desk. "You shouldn't do that, you'll get sick." His mask hid his horrified expression.

"What? You got the 'rona, Double D? You'd do me a favor. I'd get a two-week vacation out of it. Actually, I need to get it when the kids finish up their spring break. Having them home is a royal pain in my ass. Hey check it out, Michelle's heading this way... and fast."

David's neck broke out in a sweat.

Joe took a step away from the desk allowing Michelle through.

Michelle's eyes tightened and the skin outside her pink homemade "Hello Kitty" mask glowed. "David!" Hints of rose and bergamot swept across his desk as she slammed her palms down as though she arrived to a sudden epiphany. "I got one!"

Monarchs, as many as he'd seen in the eucalyptus groves in Santa Cruz, fluttered inside his stomach. His voice cracked, "Okay, Michelle, let's hear it—"

Joe snorted. "Are you guys still playing that stupid game? Michelle, just face it, you're never going to stump my man here, he's a walking computer! His brain is full of useless facts."

David sunk back into his chair.

Michelle rolled her shoulders and cracked her knuckles. "Not this time, Joe. All right, which is the correct plural form of octopus?" Michelle took a confident breath before revealing the choices. "Is it octopuses? Octopi? Octopodes? Or none of the above?"

Joe quickly answered before David. "None of the above, they're called Octopussies."

David closed his mind to Joe's cackling, then to Michelle's tempered frustration at Joe's ability to always skirt the line of office professionalism. He thought on the answer while they argued with each other. *Each is correct. The variants stem from their differing origins—Latin, English, and Greek. The answer is actually, all of the above.* He interrupted their argument, "Okay, I think I've got it."

Michelle turned her back to Joe, pressed her elbows onto the desk, and framed her face with her fingers, invading a bit more of David's personal space.

David scooted his chair an inch towards her and lost himself in her confident hazel eyes.

"So? What's the answer? You got me waiting with bated breath."

David hesitated so he could linger awhile longer in that moment. "Octopi. The answer is Octopi."

Michelle enthusiastically slammed her palms onto the desk. "Wrong! It's all of them! They're all technically correct. Some more than others, but each can be used without harassment from the grammar Nazis." Michelle mimed a mic in her hand, then dropped it onto the floor beside David's desk. "I knew I'd get you one of these days," she said while wiping a tear of laughter from her eye.

Joe slow clapped. "Congratulations, Michelle."

Michelle glared at him. "Actually, there was another reason I came by to talk to you. I was hoping I could pick your brain on an account I've been struggling with. Seems like I'm just going in circles with the numbers."

The tone shifted and David remembered who he was—a work colleague. "Yeah, sure… Michelle."

"Great. I'll swing by after lunch if that's ok with you."

"Yeah. That'd be fine."

Joe watched Michelle walk back to her desk. "Smooth, Double D. If I wasn't married—"

"She just needs my help, Joe, it's nothing more than that." David wasn't sure who he needed to convince.

"You should go for her. You're a young guy, single…" Joe eyed David from his torso to his hairline, "…and not too ugly. I mean for a dude, you've got nice eyes, and that's basically all she can see with your underwear spread out across your face."

"We're colleagues, she doesn't see anything more than that. Look, I got a lot of work I need to get back into, so if you don't mind."

"I hear you loud and clear, Double D. But I'm gonna put in a good word for you around the water cooler. Don't worry about Michelle, I got you, bro." Joe tapped his clenched fist against his heart at David then turned down the hall.

David wasn't sure why Joe talked to him. The only thing they seemed to have in common was their age and having been hired a few weeks apart from each other. He's obnoxious and loud, a little insulting, but deep down, David desperately craved his friendship. And Michelle's. She was nice to him, though he didn't feel like he deserved it. His feelings towards her were real, but constrained, like over-risen dough in a sealed bowl. He swore he'd patch the hole his ex-fiancé left in his heart before he would allow love to fill it again. When that would happen, he wasn't sure. Two years later, he still hadn't figured it out. In the meantime, passersby like his ex and Joe walked into his life and took a seat for a short spell. He'd accept whatever muck and mire they carried in with them only because he assumed they'd accept his. When they'd invariably leave, his lesson remained unlearned. As a child, he recalled begging his mother for a puppy, but instead, was gifted a toy dog—a weak simulacrum that he'd accept with abbreviated happiness until its batteries died.

David watched Joe's kids running back and forth across his screen during the morning Zoom briefing. The host spoke over the noise, "Hey, Joe... Joe... you need to click mute."

Despite transitioning the firm to work from home nearly two months ago, Joe still failed to grasp the etiquette of video conferencing. "Sorry, let me just—"

The host spoke again, "We lost you, Joe."

Joe's image went black, but his mic remained active. "Ok, let me give this a try."

A few audible mouse clicks and Joe's video feed went live. David felt relief at seeing the red slash over the icon of Joe's mic.

"Now we can get started..."

David pinned Joe's feed while he listened to the host speak. He studied the video as though it was a Norman Rockwell painting, "Portrait of a Quarantined American Family." Joe, in his bathrobe, perched in his brightly colored gaming chair sipping coffee from a mug that looked as though it hadn't been washed in a week. Tugging on his arm, his six-year-old son tried to climb onto his lap, silently whining about wanting to be in the video. In the background, Joe's wife glided back and forth across the screen—first in a towel, then a bra—apparently unaware she was being live casted to twenty of Joe's co-workers. David nearly shot coffee from his nose after watching Joe's wife slap him in the back of the head before she placed their son on his lap. Joe appeared defeated. The confidence he exuded at work seemed drained from his body. David worried Joe was unhealthy, more mentally than physically.

David opened a private chat.

Joe, you doing ok?

Hey, DD. Just tired. Kids can't go back to school. Everything's online and we're apparently their teachers now.

I'm sure they're excited to be home.

David watched Joe fan his hand across his disheveled family room littered with clothes, half eaten food, and toys. *Can't you tell?*

Joe picked up his laptop and walked it into another room.

So, DD. The misses and I are splitting up.

I'm sorry to hear that, you ok?

Yeah, just quarantining is a bitch… and it turns out she's a bitch. We're in separate rooms, just waiting for the pandemic to settle down so I can find a place to rent. Soooo, if you haven't asked Michelle out yet, you cool if I start talking to her?

David's fingers went numb. The hole in his heart ached. He shut off his video feed and typed: *brb*. But he never left his seat. He pulled the pin from Joe's feed and placed it on Michelle's. A voyeur staring into her studio apartment, he watched her take notes as the host spoke. Her apartment was exceptionally clean, decorated with bright colors, and saturated by light from an east facing window. He scanned his own apartment outside the tidied space framed by his laptop camera. Cobwebs slung across dusty rings of curtains he couldn't recall when he'd last opened. A thrift store couch, a mattress on the floor, and two milk crates in place of a coffee table—the assemblage of furniture pieced over a year and used by no one other than himself. He bit his tongue hoping the pain would bring him back to reality. He whispered a familiar affirmation to himself, "she'd never love me. It was always a pipe dream."

The host stopped mid-sentence and David's computer pinged. It was Joe: *DD, your fucking mic is hot!*

David froze. He watched Michelle pull her head up from her notes, appearing confused as to why the host stopped speaking. Even donning a quizzical expression, he thought Michelle was exceptionally beautiful. After muting his mic, he silently cried. Exhausted from subsisting in the realm of hopes and dreams and fractured hearts, he typed his reply to Joe: *She's all yours.*

The north pedestrian sidewalk of the Golden Gate bridge lacked tourists and the angry joggers who yelled at them to get out of their way. David suspected the tourists avoided the city because of the BLM rally taking place, while the locals were either sheltered in their homes or currently marching through downtown. His stomach rolled as he thought on the state of the world and his place in it. He spun his head over the rail, slipped his mask onto his forehead, and opened his mouth over the Pacific, readying to release the contents of his empty stomach, but there was nothing more to expel. In his state of emotional suffocation, he scanned the infinite horizon and deeply inhaled the salty air of the bay. He'd forgotten the taste of un-filtered air on his tongue. He freed the strain against his ears and pocketed the mask. The cold morning air bit his cheeks and nose. He realized he'd grown accustomed to the protec-tion the mask offered and felt abashedly naked without it, de-spite his intentions of being on the bridge alone that morning. The fresh air renewed his focus and he continued on.

Standing before the south tower, David took a moment to read the plaque affixed at its base. He craned his neck and mar-veled at the engineering created by the courageous and far-sighted men that built it. He followed its steel cables until he reached the bridge's midpoint, then peered over the railing onto the bay—swirling whitecaps churned beneath him.

The phone in his pocket felt like a stone. He retrieved it, and scanned the face for anything that would keep him grounded to the sidewalk. But it only offered the date and time. Before slipping it back into his pocket, he decided to text Joe: *Hey Joe, just wanted to say thanks for being my friend.* He gripped the rail, took a long breath of the salty air and pulled himself up.

Above the windsong of the Golden Gate, David's phone pinged in his pocket. He sat atop the railing and read Joe's mes-sage: *Weirdo! Hey, look, I never did reach out to Michelle. It wasn't cool of me. I'm working really hard at not being a dick, so there's bound to be some slip ups. That was one of them. No hard feelings.*

David replied: *No. No hard feelings. Take care, Joe.*

With the phone back in his pocket, he closed his eyes. He thought of Michelle, whether she'd notice he wasn't at the next Zoom meeting. He wondered why the hole in his heart didn't contract after reading Joe's text. The news should have sparked

something in him, but there was nothing but the same emptiness he'd always felt.

The fabric of his trousers tightened against his scrotum as
he leaned forward. He tried not to think about it, but the more
he moved, the tighter it got. He imagined himself dangling up-
side down by his crotch after his jeans caught on an exposed
bolt. He thought on the firefighters laughing behind their
masks as they cut him loose. His phone chirped in his pocket.
He reasoned one more hit of dopamine wouldn't hurt. It was
Joe: *Hey did you check your work email? You can get a puppy now on
the company's dime! Something about countering the depression from social
isolation.*

In the time David shifted himself in a more comfortable
spot on the railing, Joe texted a meme: Oprah standing before
her audience in a red dress, the caption below read: *You get a
puppy! And you get a puppy! Everyone gets a puppy!*

David stared at the picture, then out across the bay. He felt
his heart contract. "I… get a puppy?"

Standing six feet from the person behind and in front of him,
David eagerly waited for his chance to enter the animal shelter
after the doors opened. This was the third shelter he'd queued
at in as many days. At each one, he left empty handed, but
convinced himself that shelters running out of animals to
adopt was a good thing. But today he stood second in line and
felt confident that the odds were in his favor of finding a
puppy.

After reviewing the preliminary paperwork David filled
out, the shelter technician, Gina, introduced herself and per-
formed a brief adoption interview.

"Have you ever had a pet before?"

"No."

"Not even as a kid?"

"No, my mother wouldn't allow it."

"Do you own your home or rent?"

"I have an apartment that I rent."

"Have you contacted your landlord about your potentially adopting a pet?"

"Yes, I have. I just have to pay more rent and give him an extra security deposit."

"Can you afford to have a pet? Beyond pet rent, there's food, daycare, vet bills."

"Well, the company I work for, they're giving me a stipend to adopt a pet, since I'm working from home because of the pandemic."

"Great, a lot of companies have stepped up like that. It's a good thing for everyone. Ok, last two questions. Dog or cat? And why do you want to adopt a pet?"

David answered as quickly as he had the others, "Dog. And to have a friend."

"Ok, there's a lot of friends that need homes here, but before I take you to the kennel floor, there are some ground rules you'll have to follow."

David nodded.

"First, you must tour the entire facility. Every adoptee is special in their own way, and you may catch a spark that you wouldn't find if you picked the first pet you saw."

David nodded again. He didn't care what the rules were, he'd tour the facility ten times if it meant he'd walk out with a puppy.

"Second, I'm going to be beside you the entire time, for the safety of you and the animals."

"Of course."

"Ok then, follow me."

David was led down a hall and through large double doors that opened into an expansive space sectioned by dividing walls made of steel kennels. Runs lined the perimeter that housed bigger dogs—rottweilers, pit bulls, German shepherds— smaller dogs occupied the kennels stacked two deep, four tall, and fifteen wide. The animals seemed to sense a change in the air, and reacted by barking, yowling, or whining—anything to get the attention of the people who walked into the room.

"You've got the floor to yourself for fifteen minutes, let me know if you have any questions."

David nodded his head. His heart thumped against his chest and he wasn't sure exactly where to start. "Puppies."

"What was that?"

"I mean, do you have any puppies?"

Gina laughed. "Everyone always wants the puppies. They forget the puppies turn into the ones barking along the walls and in the kennels. Follow me, but don't forget about rule number one."

David walked along the wall of kennels. He'd never seen so many varieties of dogs in one place. He counted a row of ten Chihuahuas, amazed that no two looked alike. Their markings, color, size, shape, all different, snowflakes fallen from the same cloud.

"Ok, here are the puppies, have at it."

David spent ten minutes playing with several puppies, but something wasn't right. They were too new, too innocent. As a kid, he wanted nothing more than to have one, but now that he was older, it didn't fit.

Meandering down the line of kennels, he passed a Jack Russell—it was the only quiet dog in the building. He paused at this realization then retreated a step back.

"That's Gunther," Gina said stepping towards the kennel, "He's a sweetheart."

David studied Gunther for a minute. A brown patch of hair covered his left eye and the base of his tail, but otherwise, he was white with flecks of grey on his muzzle. His dark eyes drooped, and he seemed tired of being stared at inside his kennel.

The technician unlatched the door. The clicking metal failed to elicit a reaction in him. "He's just tired, let me get a lead on and we can take him for a walk."

With four paws on the ground, Gunther sniffed the air. David walked behind him, allowing Gunther to take him where he pleased.

"He does seem like he wants to show you something," Gina said with a coy smile, "And I think I know what."

Gunther led David to an empty kennel at the end of the dividing wall. He sniffed with deliberate focus and after seemingly overcome with a sudden realization, he turned up to Gina.

"Yup, I knew it. Isabella. They were relinquished as a pair—a Jack Russell and a bichon frise seems like an odd pair but I guess I've seen odder. The owner contracted coronavirus and sadly passed away. Her family couldn't keep any pets, so they had to give them up. We tried to adopt them as a pair, but there were no takers."

David leaned down and awkwardly patted Gunther's head.

"Actually, full disclosure," Gina skimmed through a document affixed to the clipboard she pulled from Gunther's kennel, "he does have a heart murmur. He's not on medication at the moment, but if you want to adopt him, you should get that regularly checked by a veterinarian."

Gunther grunted when David lifted him off the ground. He held him in the crook of his arm as he pressed his floppy ear against his chest. "See, I've got a hole in my heart, too."

Gunther sniffed around David's apartment.

"I know it's not much, but it's home."

Twenty paces later, Gunther finished the tour of his new den.

"You're probably hungry, let me fix you up some food." David opened the fridge—a half loaf of white bread, a jar of squeeze mayonnaise, some lunch meat, and a jar of pickles. "I guess we should hit up the grocery store after lunch, now that I'm gonna have to cook for two."

Gunther wagged his tail as David assembled their sandwich. He sliced it down the middle and placed each half on separate plates. He set his on the table and Gunther's in front of the baseboards next to the fridge. David opened his mouth to take a bite but saw Gunther, turning his nose up at his food. "I agree. Something isn't right." He took his plate and set it beside Gunther's on the floor. He sat down and leaned his back against the wall, Gunther didn't wait for him to settle before he jumped onto his lap. He held a half sandwich in each hand, offered Gunther his, while taking a bite from his own. Gunther took small bites from the sandwich David hovered in front of his muzzle while wagging his tail. "I agree, this is better."

David shut off the morning news and tossed the remote onto the coffee table. "It's a good thing you're not a kid, Gunther. You'd be forced to go back to school in the midst of a pandemic."

Gunther tilted his head to his side appearing as though he was thinking of a response when a bird swooped in and perched on the balcony outside their window. Gunther barked and sprinted at it, pawing the glass while growling at the bird.

"Buddy, try as you might, you're never gonna get that bird." David watched Gunther circling in frustration from being an arm's length away from his prize. "And your heart's gonna explode outta your chest in the process..." Despite his frustrated groans, Gunther's tail wagged furiously. "But I guess if it makes you happy, have at it... but I'm gonna give you your heart meds a little early, just in case."

David opened the fridge door. After a few minutes of shuffling food around, he found the pills. He shook the bottle and got a sense of how much was left. "A few more days, bud, then we're gonna have to beat down the postal service's door and demand they give us your refill. Nor rain, nor snow, nor sleet, nor hale... nor fascism, right, Gunny?" He placed two pills on a teaspoon and drizzled a small amount of chocolate syrup over the top. "A little high fructose corn syrup to help the medicine go down... Gunny! Num-nums!"

Gunther ignored the bird and sprinted into the kitchen.

David's phone chirped, then a minute later started ringing. David scanned the kitchen, then the living area for his phone.

He stood still, trying to pinpoint the exact location he'd last left it. "Gotcha," David retrieved it from his bedside table. *One missed call: Joe.*

"What's up, Joe?"

"Hey buddy, I really need someone to talk to. Any chance we can meet somewhere? I'll wear a mask and do the whole distancing thing, just need a face to face."

"Sure, Joe. I was planning on taking Gunther to Golden Gate Park today. Would that work for you?"

"Yeah, anywhere, I'm leaving now."

"Ok, but it'll take about ninety minutes for us to get there. How about the carousel next to Koret playground?"

"Sure, I'll be waiting. And thanks David."

"Yeah, anytime. See you soon."

Despite it being a Saturday, the playground was eerily empty. "Now Gunther, this playground would be overflowing with kids that you could befriend, but we're living in a weird time-line where playgrounds have become petri dishes."

Gunther placed one paw onto the sand, appearing unsure whether he liked the new medium or not.

"David!" Joe called out from a bench near the carousel. He slow jogged towards them.

"Good to see you in the flesh again, Joe. This is Gunther, you two haven't formally met yet."

"Cool, way cuter in person than the pictures. Hiya Gunther."

Gunther sniffed at Joe's shoe, then turned away from both of them, tightening the leash as he tried to lead them deeper into the park.

"Up for a stroll, Joe?"

"Sure."

It didn't take long for Joe to confide his misery of being alone while in the trial separation phase of their divorce. "We were high school sweethearts, married out of college. Fuck, I've never been alone, and it fucking sucks. I think I'm gonna try and reconcile."

"You could do that, but will that solve the problem of what drove you two to split up in the first place?"

Joe thought for a minute. "I guess…

it won't. Fuck. What the fuck am I supposed to do then?"

"Live alone."

"Double D, you're not hearing me, that's exactly what I don't want to do."

"You may not want to, but I think you need to. You need to learn what you had by not having it. It's like you've been living next to this fresh water lake your entire life… but I think a walk in the desert will do you some good. Shift your priorities. I think you'll figure out pretty quick the things you've taken for granted. Then, when you find yourself beside a body of water, maybe it's the same one you left, or maybe it's different, you'll respect it. Cherish it. Joe, you'll honor it."

"Fuck, Double D… that's some harsh wisdom you're dropping. But I don't think I'm strong enough for a journey like that."

David chuckled, "I know, you're not." He broke etiquette and stepped closer to Joe who hadn't noticed or seemed to care. He rested a hand on his shoulder, "but whenever you feel like you're gonna break, just lean on me."

They continued hiking through the park. Now off leash, Gunther ran across empty fields, chasing birds, and smelling wildflowers. Joe revealed more of himself during their hike, David volleyed bits of himself back. In this way, they both lost track of time, and sense of direction.

"Let me pull up a map on my phone, find out where the hell we are." Joe bent his neck down, tapping the screen of his mobile with his thumb while David snapped the leash back onto Gunther.

Gunther started barking with desperation. "What is it?" David peered ahead. In the distance, a dog paced along the edge of a grassy embankment along their path. Gunther unexpectedly lurched forward, causing the leash to slip from David's hand. "Gunther! Get back here!" David turned to Joe, "Figure it out, I'm gonna get Gunther."

David's fast walking turned into a sprint after he watched Gunther pounce on top of the other dog. The owner seemed to be struggling to hold both leashes while keeping the two dogs at bay.

"I'm so sorry! I don't know what got into him. He just bolted and the leash slipped from my hands." David spoke at a distance while still running towards them.

"It's honestly ok," the owner of the other dog called back, "They seem like they're just playing."

More at ease now, David slowed to a jog, then stopped. "Michelle?"

Michelle stood from the grass. "David? Oh my god! Crazy seeing you here. I feel like it's been ages since I've seen anyone from work that wasn't pixelated."

David got within six feet from her, "Yeah, crazy world keeps getting crazier."

"And this is your dog? I didn't even know you had one? We need to set up some play dates!"

David smiled behind his mask. "Yeah... that'd be nice." He squatted, "Gunther, what was all that about?"

"It's really all right. Isabella needed a friend."

"Did you say... Isabella?"

David sat a few feet downwind from Michelle and revealed Gunther and Isabella's origin story. Michelle admitted to adopting Isabella after learning of the company's pet stipend. "It's so crazy," she said, "their world collapsed around them, and here they are, loving on each other after being reunited." Michelle slammed her palms against the grass. "David! We need to make a pact. We can't keep them from each other, they gotta meet at least once a week. C'mon, pinky up, coronavirus be damned." She raised her pinky in the air and leaned towards him.

David met her half way and locked his pinky with hers, "I promise." He caught Joe walking towards them. Joe seemed to recognize Michelle in the distance as he slowed to a stop. He waved at them before turning around and proceeded back the way he came. A minute later, David's phone pinged in his pocket. It was a text from Joe: *The truth is, I never needed to put a good word in for you. Sayonara, Kemosabe, I'm gonna go take a walk in the desert.*

BIOGRAPHIES

Tom Altreuter is a local charlatan who continues to evade punishment for his many crimes, writing is but one example.

David Beaumier (he/him) always holds true to his first love of Argentine tango, but when not dancing he writes. His work has appeared in EWU's *Inroads*, WWU's *Suffix*, *Whatcom Writes*, and *Ham-Lit*. He's worked as the assistant publishing director at Village Books, the project manager for *The Writers' Corner* Anthology, and currently edits part time while working for The Chanticleer Book Review.

Raj Gill is an emergency veterinarian by trade. He took a few years off to travel the world and upon his return, wrote a narrative piece published by Salon magazine, How to travel the world with 2 little kids: Teach them that every step counts. Since then, he has turned his attention towards writing fiction and is currently in the revision stage of his first novel.

Molly Hite grew up in Pullman and Seattle, then moved to New York City, where she worked with the Poverty Program, listener-sponsored radio and the Women's Liberation Movement. She returned to Seattle to get degrees in philosophy and English, then became a Professor of English at Cornell University. She has published academic books and articles on modern and contemporary literatures. She has written two novels, one an academic satire and the other a police procedural. Upon retirement she moved to Bellingham, where she is working on several short stories and a novel about addiction. "Bees," a satire about the coronavirus, is her most recent story. She has two grown children and a ten-year-old genius grandson.

Dianne Meyer had a military childhood that provided a kaleido-scope of people and places. Adulthood gave her the experience of what, when, why and how. Now, retirement offers time and the means to construct these amusements. I'm having a good time and wish our readers the same.

Kenneth Meyer and his wife May are now proud residents of Washington state, but prior to 2013 he spent most of his adult life overseas, large parts of it in the Middle East and greater China area. From a young age he has had an enthusiasm for storytelling and writing.

Kim Bogren Owen, as a child, became inspired to write by *The Hobbit* and *The Lord of the Rings* trilogy. These stories, a childhood spent playing in the foothills of Colorado Springs, and working with young children became the motivation for her writing.

Armed with a BA in Anthropology, she works in the field of early childhood education although she now works educating and supporting adults at the college level. Now in addition to writing for children, she also writes for adults. She has two self-published children's books, *Art Parts: A Child's Introduction to the Elements of Art* and *Orchids*. She lives in Bellingham with her husband, two children, and three dogs. In her free time, she enjoys hiking, beach combing, photography, and will never pass up a good book.

Richard Pearce-Moses is a retired archivist. He has published several non-fiction works, including *A Glossary of Archival and Records Terminology* (Society of American Archivists, 2005). He began writing fiction in 2019 to pursue a bucket list dream of writing a science fiction novel. Covid struck four chapters into the novel, and he diverted much of his time to a short story for this anthology and sewing masks. He lives in Bellingham with his husband of thirty years, Frank Loulan.

Van Peltekian currently resides in Bellingham but is originally from the Midwest. He writes fiction primarily in prose form, but is a trained screenwriter as well. When not writing, Van's time is cut between pursuing his musical endeavors as a bass player, practicing his eye in photography, and hiking with his dog.

Nancy Sherer is a long-time resident of Bellingham, Washington. After a lifetime of adventure, politics, and social activism, she turned her attention to writing fiction. She enjoys creating characters and following them with their lives. In recent years, she has written a Y/A novel, several short stories, and is currently working on a mystery series featuring Clarity Jones.

Bob Zaslow has had three careers before retiring to write poems, plays and children's books in Sedro-Woolley, Washington: documentary filmmaker, advertising copywriter, and New York City school teacher. He won a Bronze American Film Festival award in documentary film, Clio and Effie awards in advertising, and wrote *Rap-Notes: Shakespeare's Greatest Hits* as a result of teaching his Bronx high school students *Hamlet*. He plans to publish eight children's books in 2021 and start a podcast and YouTube show.

CPSIA information can be obtained
at www.ICGtesting.com
Printed in the USA
JSHW041647070521
14456JS00001B/12